The Life of a Bishop's Assistant

Viktor Shklovsky

THE LIFE OF A BISHOP'S ASSISTANT

Translated from the Russian by Valeriya Yermishova

DALKEY ARCHIVE PRESS

Originally published in Russian by Leningrad: Kubich as *Zhitie arkhiereiskogo sluzhki* in 1931.

Viktor Shklovsky's Russian texts copyright © 2009 by Varvara Shklovskaya-Kordi
Translation rights into the English language are granted by the FTM Agency, Ltd., Russia, 2009 © English translation rights 2017
Translation copyright © 2017 by Valeriya Yermishova
First Dalkey Archive edition, 2017.

Library of Congress Cataloging-in-Publication Data
Names: Shklovskii, Viktor, 1893-1984, author. | Yermishova, Valeriya, translator.
Title: The life of a bishop's assistant / by Viktor Shklovskii; translated by Valeriya Yermishova.
Other titles: Zhitie arkhiereiskogo sluzhki. English
Description: Victoria, TX : Dalkey Archive Press, 2017.
Identifiers: LCCN 2017006133 | ISBN 9781628971743 (pbk. : alk. paper)
Subjects: LCSH: Dobrynin, Gavriil, 1752-1824--Fiction. | Clergy--Russia--Fiction.
Classification: LCC PG3476.S488 Z31513 2017 | DDC 891.73/42--dc23
LC record available at https://lccn.loc.gov/2017006133

 transcript

This publication was effected under the auspices of the Mikhail Prokhorov Foundation TRANSCRIPT Programme to Support Translations of Russian Literature.

www.dalkeyarchive.com
Victoria, TX / McLean, IL / Dublin

Dalkey Archive Press publications are, in part, made possible through the support of the University of Houston-Victoria and its programs in creative writing, publishing, and translation.

Printed on permanent/durable acid-free paper

The birth of the aforesaid

IN 1751, THE Malorussian hetman Razumovsky and the bishop Kirill, who was also quite memorable, rode through the town of Sevsk on hundreds of wagons.

In 1752, a boy was born and christened Gavriil in the family of the priest Ivan Dobrynin.

Both of the infant's grandfathers and his father were in the holy order.

His grandfather was a priest in the Sevsk district, five hundred versts from Moscow, in the Rodogozh village on the Nerussa River, and his other grandfather, who was from the other branch of the family, was a priest in the same district, in the Nevara village.

The boy grew older. In 1756, the Rodogozh grandfather went to Moscow to finish an adversarial proceeding with his rivals. And in 1757, on April 12, Ivan Dobrynin died.

Upon being notified of his son's death, the old man instantly developed a fever.

Gavriil Dobrynin wept at the Nerussa River, grieving for his dad.

He had nothing to live on. He had no choice but go live with his other granddad, the one from Nevara.

Moving in with his grandfather

AFTER MOVING TO his grandfather's house in Nevara, Gavriil lived with him for almost a year and turned six.

His grandfather ordered him to bow down to the ground thrice before an icon and they began to study the alphabet.

His instruction was brutal. People said that the child needed angelic patience to learn how to spell the word "angel."

It was an elaborate education. In accordance with the Slavic Greek Latin Academy's regulations, it consisted of a *fara*—a class where students learned to read and write in Latin—and an *infima*, which taught Slavo-Russian and Latin grammar, syntax, rhetoric, philosophy, and theology.

According to regulations, the prefect of this academy could not be too severe or melancholic.

At the academy, they studied such subjects as where angels were created, if they could bring themselves and other bodies into motion, how they thought and understood—by means of merging, differentiation, or some other way—and how big they were. But Gavriil Dobrynin did not reach that level. They say that a good start is only half the battle. It was at this half that the Nevara grandfather's work came to a halt. Meanwhile, the grandfather from Rodogozh returned from Moscow. He came to the Spassky Monastery in Sevsk for litigation with his adversaries.

Nature had endowed him with a gentle but petty heart. Hence, he wrote a letter asking that his grandson be sent to Sevsk.

But the Nevara grandfather didn't see the need to trouble himself with a messenger cart.

Gavriil's fate vacillated between the two grandfathers for a long time.

Finally, after Easter, on the tenth Friday of the year, fate had decided that Gavriil be sent to Sevsk.

There is a fair in Sevsk on that day. The priest from Nevara sent his nephew Stepan to the fair for a dry fish known as roach and bid him to take his grandson. Gavriil's mother remained with her father for the time being.

Moving from one grandfather's house to the other's

WHEN HE SAW his grandson, the Rodogozh grandfather picked him up in delight and, pressing him to his chest, called him the little branch left to him by God as consolation and other names.

By nature, grandfather was spirited, unforgiving, quick-witted, hot-tempered, enterprising, fearless in his trials, and patient in his woes.

His participation in lengthy proceedings at State offices against malicious attacks and robberies granted him knowledge of court justice; were he, moreover, educated, he would have been a State official.

Rodogozh belonged to Count Chernyshev and was governed by the Smolensk gentleman Krayevsky.

Krayevsky, who resented grandfather for his sense of initiative in legal matters and, perhaps, in love matters, grabbed him, dragged him to the stable, and brutally tortured him.

The Rodogozh grandfather's wife died young.

As a rule, a clergyman may not take a second wife and the widower must remain a monk.

They dragged grandfather to the monastery. He took his feud with Krayevsky to the monasteries.

The Rodogozh grandfather was overcome with sorrow.

Out of sorrow, he took up handicrafts—carpentry, tailoring, and weaving. In the evenings, grandfather sat under a tree with his grandson.

The monastery gates are already closed.

The under-wall passages are not for an old man, but the evening is fine.

And here, under the tree, the cloistered grandfather sang his favorite song:

Oh! How difficult it is
To live without happiness in your youth.
Sadness crushes you,
Your heart always melts with woe.
Oh, my youthful years,
Which are dearer to me than any flower!
Drift away in misfortune,
Await feeble old age;
When the color of youth passes,
You don't expect to be happy.
After spring, winter is unpleasant.
Oh! Our life is so erratic!
In old age, there is no peace,
Only illness and misfortune;
At least there was happiness then,
It's not so pleasant in old age!
Happiness, where are you dwelling?
Or are you living with the beasts?
Quit living with the beasts, happiness,
And come serve poor me.

The meaning of these verses is understandable.

Gavriil lived in the monastery under his grandfather's tutelage for almost three years and learned not only to read, but even to write.

Upon hearing of this education, the archimandrite gave Gavriil his old justicoat, which was made of green nankeen with cotton wadding.

The caftan was altered and Gavriil, too, began to resemble an archimandrite.

This archimandrite was named Innokentiy Grigorovich. He was one of the treasurers of the Trinity Lavra of St. Sergius. And, after serving in Sevsk, he was transferred to the Vysotsky Monastery in Serpukhov.

An interregnum began at the monastery.

There is a Greek word, *stómachos*.

It means digestive tract.

And there is a message from Apostle Paul to Timothy: "Do not drink water, but partake of a bit of wine, for your stomach."

By virtue of this text, the monks drank for their digestive systems. Holy scripture is a wise thing.

For example, there are prescriptions for fasts.

There is another precept: a guest may not turn down food, even non-vegetarian food. Hence, whenever the stomach requires non-vegetarian food, the monks visit each other's cells.

They eat, they drink.

It was on one such evening that old monk Iliodor quarreled with Gavriil's grandfather.

After this quarrel, grandfather went to sleep and laid down his grandson beside him. But the monk was not forgetful.

When they blew out the candle and everyone went to sleep, the monk picked up a log and went into grandfather's room.

Gavriil took the blow.

Gavriil began to scream.

They turned the lights back on and everyone awoke.

During the interregnum, the monastery was ruled by its treasurer, Father Savva Trebartensky. The hearing took place at night. They roused the other monastery elder, Varfolomey, and went around the rooms with lanterns. The monk was seized— the beating of his heart gave him away. He resorted to denial.

Grandfather insisted that the black-robed one be interrogated under torture or else he would write such a denunciation that the next day, the judges and the accused would both be sent to the Sevsk provincial chancery. The judges were frightened by such words spoken in anger. The key-keeper was completely illiterate and grandfather kept the treasurer's receipts and expense books and knew all of the monastery's business.

An interrogation under torture is an interrogation in the

torture chamber, which is also known as the mossless baths.

It was conducted on a rack—a hanging device. A log was tied to a person's legs and an executioner stood on top of it.

They drew a bundle of burning birch twigs down the interrogated's back and beat him with a whip.

They took him off the rack and straightened his arms.

They tortured him thrice and this was known as serving three masses.

The torture was not considered punishment—only a means of finding out the truth.

This was why the judges became frightened and turned the monk over to grandfather.

The monk threw himself at grandfather's feet.

Grandfather insisted that, according to monastic rules, the monk must be punished by monastic rosaries, which consisted of heavy globes strung on a rope almost an arshin long. The culprits were beaten with these rosaries while the penitential psalm was recited slowly thrice.

The monk begged for mercy and, to avoid a greater evil, asked to be shackled with a chain. They resolved to place a chain and a sling on the offender and imprison him in an empty tower for a week, thus ending the proceeding.

The monastery shackles were heavier than twenty-four kilograms and the sling was a band with a heavy lateral metal stick.

The sling prevented one from lying down or standing up.

The monk sat in the tower; nobody knows what songs he sang there.

Meanwhile, a new archimandrite arrived, the elder Pakhomiy.

He was so old that he was ancient. He barely had enough time to settle into his chambers when a great uprising took place among the monks. The uprising took place on account of two clauses.

Owing to his old age, Pakhomiy did not invite the friary over for vodka.

Pakhomiy eliminated the Saturday baking of blini and the Sunday baking of pies.

The monastery's altar boy Semyon Malyshev took it upon himself to draft the denunciation. Despite his youth, this character rivaled the Rodogozh grandfather in reputation and was considered no less adept in carrying out orders. He acquired this skill while on the run and living in the town of Kineshma as a servant to the local military commander, whom he slandered all the way to the Secret Chancery.

This experienced creature assured the monks that the archimandrite was an enemy of God and should be squealed on under the first and second articles.

The first and second articles usually represented the word and the deed.

The first article pertained to an individual who was guilty of insulting God and the Church.

The second article pertained to insulting the sovereign and breaching State ordinances.

The Secret Chancery was established to enforce these very two articles.

The Secret Chancery was a place whose name alone caused people to faint.

While listening to the scheme, the boy didn't understand what a first and second article were and assumed that the first article was a ban on baking blini and the second—on baking pies, thinking the crime terrible. The altar boy Malyshev was brave and accustomed to hanging on the rack, given that the informer was also tortured in those times.

He ran into the Sevsk provincial chancery and started shouting "word and deed."

Pursuant to the laws, they placed shackles on the archimandrite's sunset years and sent the witnesses to the Secret Chancery along with the informer (all the monks served as witnesses).

Here, critical new information emerged. It turned out that, during the Vespers held on the festive occasion of the Sovereign Empress's Name Day, the archimandrite bid his acolytes to recite the canticles rather than sing them.

Semyon Malyshev was sentenced to corporal punishment and drafted into the army, while the archimandrite was ordered to sing without being able to invoke his old age and gout.

The expedition, or the proceeding thus ended, it did not leave the crafty, enterprising, unforgiving, spirited, and fearless Rodogozh grandfather above suspicion.

The archimandrite requested that the Moscow Metropolitan issue an order to also transfer this crafty informer and his legal dispute to the Nikolayevsky monastery in Stolbov, which was located fifty versts from Sevsk. Gavriil, who by then was ten years old, followed his grandfather there.

Sojourn in the Stolbov monastery

THE STOLBOV MONASTERY is located seven versts from Rodogozh.

The archimandrite Varlaam Mayevsky, who received the spirited, unforgiving, enterprising, and fearless grandfather Dobrynin in his monastery, was afraid of him and expected nothing good from Gavriil either.

Therefore, he sent the old man to the Rodogozh hermitage, out of sight. And kept Gavriil Dobrynin as a kind of hostage. By that time, Gavriil already had a voice—a treble. He could thus reimburse the archimandrite for his living expenses.

Expulsed to the hermitage (as the small monasteries without archimandrites or superiors were called), grandfather could no longer lodge a complaint against the archimandrite pursuant to the first or second article.

Gavriil's mother was admitted to the veil and settled at the Sevsk nunnery.

At the Stolbov monastery, the monks often called Gavriil into their cells, admiring his comeliness while they instructed him to love virtue and become worthy of the angelic rank.

All the monks there thought themselves to hold that rank, including the grandfather from Rodogozh.

Once, after the evening prayer in church, one of the monks, Father Arseniy, took advantage of the archimandrite's absence and hopped off the left choir-place, raising his mantle and leaping around the church like a monkey, but in time with the ecclesiastical chanting.

Naturally and understandably, Arseniy was drunk.

The monk's leaping amused Gavriil. He thought that it brightened the entire Vespers.

Gavriil thought that if he recounted this spectacle to the archimandrite, perhaps he would ask Father Arseniy to leap some more for everyone's entertainment and make this a ritual at Vespers.

But after listening to Gavriil, the archimandrite reasoned otherwise—he sent Father Arseniy to the monastic kitchen to chop wood and carry water.

As a result, the monks began to detest Gavriil, believing him, and not unjustly, to be an informer.

The archimandrite grew to love the boy and asked him to reenact the spectacle of the leaping monk numerous times in his cell, laughing heartily and clapping his hands.

Then, on July 28, 1762, a historic event took place. Emperor Peter was overthrown by the Empress and died a few days later, of colic, they said.

The joy of the Imperial Guard, which had appointed Catherine Empress, was immeasurable.

Every kind of wine there was in the capital, including grain wine and grape wine, was consumed.

Rumor had it that the villages would be returned to the monasteries. Rumor had it that Orlov would become Tsar.

Other rumors abounded.

They were spoken of in the monasteries and whispered about in the streets.

But in early July, a drum began to beat in the streets and the following manifesto was read.

"We decree that each and every one of our loyal subjects adhere solely to their title and occupation, abstaining from any insolent and indecent statements. But against all expectations and to our great regret and displeasure, we hear that there are people of such depraved morality and ideas that they do not consider the common good and peace, but are themselves infected with strange beliefs about matters that do not concern them at all and who, without having any direct knowledge of such matters, try to infect the other feeble-minded . . . If the present maternal exhortation and solicitude has no effect on the hearts of the depraved and does not return them to the path of true bliss, then each of these ignoramuses must know that we will act with the full severity of the law."

In short, people were ordered to keep quiet and prosper.

Before long, however, Gavriil was transferred from the Stolbov monastery to the Rodogozh hermitage.

The grandson meets his crafty grandfather again

THE BOY LIVED with his grandfather for three years, learning to sing from sheet music and do arithmetic.

Grandfather calculated the monastery's wholly unprofitable financial situation on paper and Gavriil's dreams of obtaining angelic rank evaporated.

Sometimes, the boy traveled to the spiritual administration bureau in Stolbov to help their clerk write the ecclesiastical news on who attended and who didn't attend confession.

At this time, the Sevsk diocese was established and the Spassky monastery in Sevsk was transformed into a bishop's house, while the Rodogozh hermitage and many other monasteries were destroyed.

Dobrynin's education was far advanced and he was reading many books, including *The Story of Gil Blas de Santillane* by Monsieur Lesage and a shorter work by the same author titled *The Bachelor of Salamanca, or Memoirs of Don Cherubim de la Ronda.*

In *The Bachelor of Salamanca*, a man sought his fortune in the service of the Bishop of Mexico.

But how does one get to Mexico from Rodogozh?

In 1765, the Rodogozh grandfather took his grandson, the so-called Russian Gil Blas, to Sevsk to find him a place in the consistory.

But the consistory—or ecclesiastical chancery—was already fully staffed.

Again, they needed to find an occupation or a course of study for him. At the time, there were no public academies in Russia. The closest seminary was five hundred versts away, in Moscow.

And it was only good because there wasn't one better.

While Gavriil Dobrynin's mysterious fate toiled on his behalf, he went to Count Chernyshev's estate office every day to improve his writing.

All in all, the estate offices of upper-class gentlemen emulated State governments; it was as if they really were such governments.

The estate trustee, clerk, and overseer acted as said government officials, while the feudal scribe played the role of secretary.

And all of them, except for the trustee, were Chernyshev's serfs.

The office consisted of two clean chambers and was sectioned off into either tables or *povytya.*

The word *povytya* is archaic, but has survived in Russia for a long time thanks to the derivative word for steward, *povytchik*. At the very least, you may have encountered it in Gogol's *Dead Souls*.

The judge's table behind the railing was covered with red fabric. On top of it lay Tsar Alexey Mikhailovich's Code and the Count's orders and forms for ruling the estate.

Wealthy peasants governed the estate through intermediaries and did as they pleased there.

A picture of the royal family and a general map of the estate hung on the wall.

A large-scale map lay by the wall, rolled up in a log that was expressly hollowed out for it.

Across from the office was a storage room for monetary contributions, the sentry room, and the archive.

It was at this academy that Dobrynin developed his talents under his grandfather's supervision. He would also set off on his trips from here.

On May 8, 1766, they drove out to the eradicated Stolbov monastery for St. Nicholas Day, which took place on the day of the fair.

As a rule, fairs were held on monastery land and were intended to coincide with monastic holidays, or the monastic holidays were intended to coincide with the fairs.

Taking an inkpot and paper with him, Dobrynin, too, drove out for the holiday. Familiar with all the customs, he rushed into the church and stood by the window. The pilgrims that crowded the church were praying continuously, hiring the monks.

They started coming up to Gavriil and asking him to write down names on cards designated for health and for the repose of a soul.

Gavriil began to diligently assist with the prayer service in return for voluntary payments. In a few hours, he felt the weight of a few copper *grivnas* in his pocket.

This exacerbated his keenness and induced him to raise the price, which, however, could not deter fervent praying hearts from carrying out their good intentions.

The devout frowned, but paid; thus, time passed—or, rather, flew by.

Time flew by, leaving Gavriil Dobrynin with memories of St. Nicholas Day and the fifty kopecks he collected from the devout.

At the time, it was not an insignificant sum.

Acts of fate

UPON RETURNING HOME from Stolbov, Gavriil was summoned by the Bishop of Sevsk, Tikhon Yakubovsky.

Because word of Gavriil Dobrynin's treble voice and sweet nature had already spread throughout the Sevsk estate office and to the Bishop's chambers.

The very same old monk Iliodor who once struck the boy with a log had at present become a priest and the Bishop's spiritual guide.

This elder, who was not vindictive and foresaw how far Gavriil could go as an offshoot of a root like the Rodogozh grandfather, informed him that he could arrange a meeting for him with the Bishop. Upon paying the cell guard ten kopecks, the supplicants were admitted to see His Grace.

His Grace was sitting in a gilded wooden armchair, wearing an ornamental robe the color of dark cherry and a green brocade cassock.

A *panagia*—a not-too-bright, round holy icon the size of a copper nickel—was hanging on His Grace's neck.

And the supplicants kneeled before this pillar of Eastern Orthodoxy.

His Grace uttered in a low voice:

"Ah! This is the boy so many have told me about. Why haven't you brought him to me a long time ago? I have appointed him choirboy."

Good-bye to the dream of becoming the Bachelor of Salamanca, good-bye to the dream of a sword and a feathered hat . . .

Angel wings—the angelic rank—flashed over Dobrynin's head.

The word "choirboy" struck Dobrynin like thunder, his countenance turned gloomy and tears rolled down his face.

Observing this, the Bishop called the boy over and asked him why he was crying.

"I never studied musical notes and am thus unfit to be a choirboy," Dobrynin sobbed, concealing his knowledge of sheet music. "I'd like to work at the consistory, with a quill in hand."

Then, the Bishop ordered Dobrynin to write the following words out on a piece of paper on a small table in the room.

"The guide of wisdom and giver of meaning, the Father's word Christ the God."

"Your writing isn't bad," His Grace said. "But you must learn that which you do not know. My secretary can read sheet music, I can sing from sheet music, and even you, after you learn how to read sheet music, may, in time, become a secretary in my consistory."

A treble-voiced choirboy was called in and they were ordered to sing a canticle by St. Dmitry of Rostov, "My beloved Jesus, sweetness for the heart," as a trial.

Although Dobrynin played coy, he could not conceal his voice. Hence, a clerk was called in and ordered to write, on behalf of Gavriil, a request to appoint him where His Grace would see fit.

The following decision was written out:

"The regent, the Reverend Father Palladiy, must train the supplicant, keeping him under particularly close watch and care."

With this cruel decree, the boy and his grandfather were led to see Father Palladiy.

And here, on the table, the boy saw a bottle of vodka.

"A three-leafer," the Rodogozh grandfather said cheerfully.

"A three-leafer, or a trefolium. Learn it, boy," Father Palladiy said. "This herb can be used to treat scurvy and can serve as an appetizer."

Every morning, His Grace Tikhon Yakubovsky came out of his private chambers into the Cross Room. Here, he gave everyone his general benediction, whereupon the choir sang *Ispolla eti despotai*, or "Blessed be the Bishop for many years."

Everyone who needed to see him entered the "admission room"—the room where the Bishop received guests. The Bishop usually sat on the admission room sofa and gave hearings, calling in his guests one by one and, most of the time, instantly pronouncing and writing down his decisions and resolutions.

Many came with complaints about each other, while others were summoned as a result of some passionate act, which the Bishop somehow learned about. In these cases, the punishments varied, of course: the guilty were reprimanded more or less severely, were assigned to menial labor in the Bishop's house or were sent to the monastery; but, very often, they also received corporal punishment right here, in the admission room, before everyone's eyes, in order to set an example.

"Hey! You troublemaker! (or 'quarreler' or 'scoundrel')," the Bishop would exclaim. "I'll teach you a lesson. Hey!" he added, turning to his servants, "Bring some whips here!"

Coachmen or other servants would show up unfailingly and without delay, carrying the two-tail whips.

"Now then, take off your clothes and lie down," the accused was told.

It was customary for the guilty party to take off all his clothing and remain in his undergarments. Now, too, he undressed and stretched out on the floor. Only two of the Bishop's servants appeared with whips for the corporal punishment, and the present clergymen, who were either assigned by the Bishop or selected by the servants, had to hold him down. They could not refuse.

Four of them instantly fell to their knees to hold his body in the shape of a cross, two holding the legs and two holding the arms; they uncovered body parts to which the two-tail whips could cling. The accused lay so that the Bishop could see with his very eyes, without getting up from the sofa, whether the whips clung closely to his body. The most whipped were the clerks, followed by the deacons; the priests, especially the young ones, were not shown lenience either.

In addition to such punishments, financial penalties were common. On account of these, Tikhon Yakubovsky prospered. For his birthday on July 16, he ordered that a pond be dug up in the shape of his monogram, TY.

The pond was dug up by priests expiating their guilt.

It was lined with multicolored stones around the banks and planted with flowers.

Father Palladiy was asked about Dobrynin's triumphs in the *partes* church choir. He replied that the student read sheet music very well. This was followed by an order to have an overcoat of thin green fabric sewn for the treble-voiced that would be unlike any other.

This overcoat was the envy of all the choirboys, who even nicknamed Gavriil "the Secretary."

Dobrynin did not abandon his old dream of becoming a man of the quill. Consequently, His Grace ordered that he move out of the choir room and live with the treasurer to assist the treasurer's clerk. Dobrynin was charged with inscribing the priests' and deacons' printed documents. In the spaces between the lines, these documents were inscribed with the name of the newly-consecrated priest or deacon and the place and name of the church where he was consecrated, as well as the date; the Bishop himself would sign below in due form.

These inscriptions afforded Dobrynin an income of approximately sixty rubles a year without depriving him of his earnings as a choirboy.

Thus, Gavriil radiated good health. He did not concern himself with any—often futile—forethought or planning.

He read Lesage and Mr. Sumarokov and quietly blossomed, like a flower in a hothouse.

On a noteworthy new face—Kirill Fliorinsky, the Bishop in ringlets

IN EARLY 1768, the oh-so-discreet Tikhon Yakubovsky was transferred to the Voronezh diocese for a sabbatical and Kirill Fliorinsky was appointed to his position as Bishop of Sevsk.

When the latter arrived, he directly gave Dobrynin a sticharion, thus endowing Gavriil with, so to say, a more official uniform and role in the church service.

Now, during the sacraments, he was supposed to hold a book before the Bishop and unfurl a round rug known as a hassock under His Grace's feet, as well as pass him a pastoral staff.

The sticharions were cut from different fabrics, which rather pleased Gavriil.

Kirill Florinsky, or Fliorinsky, as he whimsically called himself, was the son of a Cossack from the Pereyaslavsky District. He studied at the Kiev Theological Academy and then became a choirboy at the Empress's court. But not for long.

Meanwhile, the position of choirboy at Elizabeth's court offered many opportunities for advancement. But Kirill, despite his not-so-diminutive height and Ukrainian origin, which was fashionable at court at the time, did not obtain any.

The distraught Kirill began to attend physics lectures at the Academy of Sciences.

Then, in 1756, he took monastic vows and was first sent

to work as a teacher in the Novgorod seminary, later serving for four years in the ambassadorial church in Paris, where he became fully fluent in French, adopted the fashions, and unsettled his nervous system.

In 1764, Kirill returned to Moscow as a result of a quarrel.

There, owing to his large build, he caught the fancy of Empress Catherine, but only as a preacher, and obtained the rank of Bishop of Sevsk and Bryansk.

This archpriest, a frequenter of Parisian high society, ordered that, during the sacraments, all the young men were coiffed with frisettes—curls covered with facial powder.

It was difficult for him to teach this to the fossilized monastery establishment.

An avid reader of novels in translation, Gavriil Dobrynin had a propensity for neatness that bordered on dandyism, and always cheered up the archpriest with his coiffure.

Ardent, haughty, and fiery-tempered, Fliorinsky had a resolute spirit and a keen intelligence.

His primary gifts were oratorical ability and a good memory. Moreover, he knew the French and Latin languages. But his longing for Paris and his pontifical occupations, which were incompatible with his remembrances, lent a whimsy to Fliorinsky's character.

There was a custom in the Bishop's house that the Bishop would send the clergymen and acolytes taking vows to the most honorable and distinguished monks for instruction in reading, writing, and ecclesiastical law.

And they were not consecrated until their teachers issued a document testifying to their progress. The right to issue such documents could raise a teacher's earnings to two hundred rubles.

Thanks to his aptitude for coiffing his hair, Gavriil, too, joined the ranks of the distinguished monks, though he was barely twenty. Gavriil immediately lowered the prices and the consecrated went to study with him in droves.

This was a complex and litigious matter because taking money for consecration was forbidden by special orders. This explained why monks accepted money, but could only quarrel about it discreetly.

And here, the full extent of Gavriil Dobrynin's cunning manifested.

His Grace loved to expound on the psalter to churchgoers.

Kirill spoke clearly and concisely and loved listening to himself, even closing his eyes from pleasure and slightly tilting his head to the side as he enunciated.

Standing at the altar, Gavriil thought of writing down the Bishop's most curious statements in his notebook.

A few days later, it occurred to Gavriil to pretend to forget his notebook on the windowsill as the Bishop passed.

Fliorinsky studied his notes, which were written in good handwriting. His face exuded pleasure. He called Gavriil over and said:

"He is not only learned if he has studied many sciences, but also if he lives attentively. I see the latter in you. Continue as you have begun, write down every word I say not only in public sermons, but also in everyday conversations, as I have so much knowledge that no one can teach me anything now."

Thus Kirill Fliorinsky praised himself. After hearing such words, Dobrynin didn't let a quill and notebook out of his hand in his presence. "Remember," he told himself, "your teacher studied in Paris, where travelers say that mules are turned into horses."

Chapter dedicated to the description of Paris, wherein, the sail of this story swells with sighs

IN THE MONTH of May, His Grace went to the city of Kiev, on a pilgrimage, so to speak.

The road was long.

The travelers were in no hurry.

In the Brovary, eighteen versts away from Kiev, His Grace awaited his carriage.

He could already see the monastery, which sat on a cliff like a tilted crown.

The golden stones of church cupolas adorned this crown.

The azure Dnieper River flowed past the white city.

In a brisk whisper, the Deacon told the Bishop about an incident on the road.

Kirill wasn't listening.

The monastery stood there in the distance like a white wreath.

The bishop stood there, thinking of the dark rooms of the seminary, his seminary studies in the city, St. Petersburg, the palace, and his misfortunes.

"So what do you think, Your Grace?" the Deacon asked.

"Ah, Paris!" the Bishop said incongruously and, looking grim, went off to his overnight lodgings. The Deacon hurried after him.

"We'll spend the night here," Kirill said.

The night was dark and quiet. Gavriil was sleeping in the foyer and suddenly heard someone call out to him in a low voice. The large, whitewashed room occupied by the Bishop was lit dimly by a candle.

The green padded brocade blanket appeared black in the candlelight.

Kirill sat in a dressing gown.

"The bedbugs are biting me," he said. "Show me your hands: do you have your notebook with you? You don't have to take notes right now.

"The sight of Kiev, young man, awoke in me memories of the seminary, and those memories brought me to the gates of Paris. I can't leave them.

"The bedbugs are biting me, I can't sleep. City gates, there are no such gates in Paris except for the Arc de Triomphe. The capital, like the heart of the French, is never closed.

"'Come,' it says to all the peoples on the face of the earth. 'Come, the black, the white, and the free, and, surrounded by the love of the most deserving women and the most amiable of men and free from the threat of inquisition, experience pleasure at any moment of your existence.'

"'Come, I have neither shutters nor guards to keep you away; my lovely call is heard in every corner of the world and the Indian, Turk, Sicilian, and Russian are running, gasping for breath, abandoning their rights and becoming Parisian residents.'

"Don't write this down, don't remember it.

"Oh Paris, oh beautiful glass houses! From every angle, I see only chandeliers and glass windows—coffeehouses. There are believed to be nine hundred of them in Paris. There are those that resemble courthouses and, in some, the ultimate verdicts on essays and writers are given. Still others are respected for their political cabinets, and that is where people study the news as they would an algebra book.

"In Paris, people of every status are needed: doctors, doll-makers, even girls of standard moral virtue.

"These girls, like rowers, turn their backs to their fate and row toward it.

Parisian coaches transport the most beautiful women from place to place with the greatest discretion, avoiding onlookers.

"Icarus's mishap took place because he was not a resident of Paris. Because Parisian air can lift you up.

"Their hairnets are the same color as their dress.

"Oh, young man, nothing is as pleasant in this world as to dare to do everything. Those fashions are charming. Those fashionable goods are music for the eyes, a harpsichord of flowers. A prelate, or priest, wears fashionable dress and takes a curtained coach from his house to an amorous rendezvous.

"Night falls and Paris appears no less dazzling. Rows of refracted lights create the most delightful illumination by the Seine and the next day, the sun will come up for the sole purpose of lighting up the most beautiful pathways leading to the most enchanting suburbs, where lovely houses abound.

"And what ingenuity, what horses, what a variety of horse sets! Only sturgeons aren't harnessed to Parisian coaches."

Kirill fell silent.

Gavriil, too, was silent, thinking of God knows what. Perhaps of the beauty of Paris and perhaps about Kiev, whose domes began to gleam behind the dim glass of the windows.

"It would be preferable," Kirill said, "if all the bell towers in Paris were gilded. Furthermore, it would befit French grandeur and add variety to the city.

"The architecture in Paris is becoming cheerier, so to speak, experimenting fancifully with the appearance of houses.

"Parisian buildings may be called comely freaks.

"The architecture there is as free as the writing: the buildings are approved by neither a chief of police nor a bishop. The writer's quill turns as fast as the tongue there and anyone can expect to be sworn at, merely for laughter's sake, because the French are not malevolent.

"Now, let us talk about time. A week is only a day in Paris, like a day is an eternity at our monastery. Everything there is traced out, printed, and publicized. Given the multitude of events, a month is worth an entire year . . ."

It was growing lighter; the Kiev domes were gold and russet on the white, tilted crown on the head of the green Kiev-Pechersky hill.

The sky was turning blue. The candlelight in the room had vanished.

Kirill fell into a reverie.

"Young man," he said. "Comb yourself for tomorrow. Remember that the cruelest tyranny in Paris is the tyranny of the friseurs, and everybody obeys them. As for everything else, keep mum. The Bastille is the only subject on which Parisian residents keep mum."

Kiev

HOWEVER SLOW MONASTERY time was, morning came a few hours later.

His Grace's arrival in Kiev was celebrated by the ringing of bells at the Monastery of the Caves.

The next day, His Grace and his entire retinue followed the supervisor of the caves to pay homage to the holy relics stored in those dark, windy underground corridors.

The long passage with the underground alcoves, from under the vaults of which, they say, the souls of saints ascended to the heavenly settlement, was an astonishing sight.

In the grooves lining both sides of it, in small coffins, lay the bodies of saints, which were likely contorted from the close quarters.

In one of those coffins in the wall even hung the incorruptible body of an infant from among those killed in Bethlehem. His journey to the Kiev-Pechersky monastery was unknown.

The Kiev Metropolitan gave the Sevsk bishop a royal welcome. Other monastery leaders received him with a humility customary of clergymen.

One day, Kirill went to visit the academic classes he had once attended.

Students from the rhetorical and theological courses, who wore grim caftans without any pants, surrounded Fliorinsky, wishing to enter into a theological discussion with him.

One of the rhetoricians approached the Bishop and asked the following:

"If a Turk and a Jew are drowning along with a Christian,

which of them should be saved first?"

The Bishop answered distractedly:

"Whoever's within reach."

This answer produced a great commotion in the crowd.

In the meantime, the Bishop demanded that they bring him the academic journal for the year he studied poetry and summoned the archimandrite Karpinsky.

Then, straightening out the journal, he found a mark inscribed by the teacher Karpinsky.

The mark was unfavorable to the student Fliorinsky and retained him in the same class for another term. The gray-bearded archimandrite stood red-faced before the eparch.

With the impetuousness of a seminarian, the eparch pronounced:

"Your mark is false, it spoils the entire transcript. I won't remove it, let it be a testament to your weakness. This mark resulted from the fact that, when I passed you, Father, I didn't bow down to you twenty-five years ago. But recalling Holy Scripture, which teaches not to repay evil with evil or insult with insult, I will content myself with a mere reprimand and release you without a whipping."

Kirill Fliorinsky's ability to hold a grudge was truly astounding.

He performed his pontifical service with his usual grandeur. Numerous priests assisted in the service.

The pomp of the Bishop's robes and the light of the double and triple candlesticks, known as *dichirias* and *trichirias*, magnified the splendor of the service. Special fans depicted the Holy Spirit over the Bishop's head.

Heavy brocade robes engulfed him with their radiance, but a fiery temper did not leave the heart of the disenchanted Parisian.

At the altar, he lit one monk's beard on fire with a *trichiria* and tore out a tuft of another's hair; he punched one in the teeth and kicked another in the gut.

He did all this while swearing profusely at the entire church.

He especially raged while he was being attired in sacred garments.

It may be said that, in those moments, he resembled a brave warrior fighting off his enemies.

Kiev priests, who weren't subject to his authority, avoided Kirill's service, fearing for their personal safety.

And it was difficult to recognize in the furious man at the altar the gloomy Parisian who reminisced about the global city that night in the Brovary.

Consecration bureau

THE TRUST ACCORDED to Gavriil was bearing fruit.

By coiffing his hair and covering his ringlets with a hairnet that matched his dress, he drew to him the heart of the tempestuous Bishop.

In Sevsk, the Bishop established a bureau and, calling it the "consecration bureau," bid the sacristan to be an attendant and Dobrynin a clerk.

The rates at the bureau were as follows.

For sorting out a case, teaching catechism, or writing a document or a letter and the like—seven rubles.

Five rubles from deacons and three rubles and fifty kopecks from candidates for priesthood consecrated into sticharions, with a view to dividing the collected sum among the choirboys in a few months' time.

The rates were handwritten by the Bishop and nailed to the bureau's wall so that Gavriil could personally enforce them.

This business seemed blameless to the Bishop, as it relieved supplicants from having to pay heavy bribes with a small price. Despite its sanctity, however, the tariff contravened the manifesto of 1746, which decreed, during the Bishop's tour of the diocese in wagons, that no money be solicited from the clergy for any reason. And that two rubles be collected from priests and one ruble from deacons for consecration.

The monk-priest Irinarch, who knew Latin, taught catechism to all the candidates for priesthood and deaconhood.

It was Irinarch who collected the Bishop's fee from the consecrated.

As for Dobrynin, he was ordered to certify all those consecrated into sticharions in the subjects of reading, writing, canon law, and catechism, and to sign their certificates.

Upon certification, each candidate had to place three rubles and fifty kopecks in a cup and as much as he wanted in the hand.

And everyone placed something in the hand for expedience.

This was why Dobrynin had proper linen and dress and provoked cruel indignation and jealousy in the Bishop's entire staff and, particularly, his secretary.

That year, it pleased His Grace to personally teach Dobrynin, his cell attendant, and two other choirboys Latin and arithmetic.

Dobrynin understood that studying under the Bishop wouldn't be easy; he therefore sought out a merchant in town who had kept books for a wine tax collector but was dismissed for drunkenness to teach him arithmetic.

Dobrynin kept this instructor well lubricated and thus learned to count, add, subtract, multiply, and divide.

Thus, Dobrynin always appeared before the Bishop with the correct solutions to assignments while his fellow classmates would, instead of giving the answer, stretch their hands out so that the arch-teacher could hit them with a small wooden shovel called a *palya*.

When they got up to calculating the square root and the cubic root, the Bishop proceeded to use a visual teaching method and instructed them to make an appropriately sized wooden cube.

The Bishop often threw this geometric figure at the forehead of the slow-witted pupil; moreover, everyone was ordered to instantly retrieve it from beneath the chair, the canapé, or the small tables, if it rolled under there, and hand it to the arch-teacher.

Thus, calculating the cubic root in the Bishop's chambers resembled a ballgame. The cubic root wasn't yet definitively calculated when snow fell on the ground. And the Bishop traveled to the towns of Rylsk, Belopolye, and other settlements to survey the diocese.

He needed to go to the best monasteries to rest, feast, and receive presents.

In Rylsk, the Bishop lectured the populace on persecuting Old Believers and, right there and then, before everyone, ordered that one of the Old Believers, retired officer Sisoy Voropanov, have his head shaved and his beard cut off with scissors.

They say that Voropanov's hair grew back upon the Bishop's departure.

After listening to the Bishop's speech with Christian patience, the merchants treated him to a hearty luncheon, beer, honey, and good liqueurs while remaining steadfast to their old faith and trade.

As for Gavriil, he wrote down the Bishop's speeches and collected payments from candidates for consecration because the Bishop continued to work during his travels.

They stationed their horses at no charge, paid nothing for grub, and everyone singing and standing before them offered them prodigious and opulent favors.

Name Day

JANUARY EIGHTEENTH WAS His Grace's Name Day.

With his earnings, Gavriil Dobrynin had himself a new set of robes sewn. In the morning, he went to wish His Grace a happy Name Day attired in these robes. Seeing Gavriil in European dress, the Bishop asked:

"Have you acquired these a long time ago?"

"In time for Your Grace's Name Day," Dobrynin replied.

After giving his benediction to everyone and dismissing them, Fliorinsky sat down on the canapé and told Gavriil the following:

"Listen, Dobrynin, you know that I'm having a lot of guests to lunch today; you know how much I like order and you know how impatient I am when I see disorder; judge and behold: can I be calm on this present day? You know that my cell monk Vasilyev, on whom this entire order depends, loves to drink to excess; a human being is no imam. Another among my brethren, a Russian bishop, would find me unfeeling, but I am a Frenchman. I didn't have the chance to be in Paris for long, but I will not and do not wish to lose the sense of Parisian order and cleanliness. Under such circumstances, I will need your services, which you should begin this present day in place of my cell monk. I hope that, even on this occasion, you will oblige me no less than you have until now."

Dobrynin replied that, though he pleaded lenience for his inexperience, he accepted the archpriest's proposition and would take pains not to infringe on Parisian rules.

Thereupon taking Dobrynin by the hand, the Bishop led him to his study and entrusted the cupboard with silverware and the linen chest to him.

Dobrynin assumed dictatorial powers and summoned from the consistory two clerks, a solicitor, two under-clerks, and two copyists.

The solicitor was ordered to remain in the kitchen and note every dish so that it wouldn't wander off and end up in some monk's cell rather than on the Bishop's table—a ruse Dobrynin had availed himself of earlier.

Dobrynin charged himself with the buffet. The rest of the regiment was responsible for serving the dishes.

Almost fifty people sat at the luncheon table.

The honor of the Bishop's home had to be upheld. Hence, calling the military commander's valet into the buffet, Dobrynin asked:

"What do proper gentlemen drink when they leave the table?"

The valet replied:

"After lunch, proper gentlemen drink coffee, but coffee service should include dessert for the guests." But where to find coffee in the Bishop's house?

The acolytes who were gathered to unearth the coffee confirmed that there was indeed coffee. But only the cell monk Vasilyev knew where it was stored.

The cell monk Vasilyev was immediately found and brought in. But it turned out that, after encountering shot glasses in the cupboard, he turned to them like a compass turns north and charged at them like Don Quixote de la Mancha charged at the puppets reenacting a chivalrous play.

A good many glasses were broken while others lay on the floor, emptied and overturned.

All attempts to talk to Vasilyev proved unsuccessful.

He spoke at length, but incoherently.

After a general search, the coffee was finally found.

However, the high society ladies had already gone home and, left in male company, His Grace became more interested in spiced wine.

The candles had already been brought in and a feeling of pleasant restfulness took hold of all the guests.

His Grace called Gavriil and said:

"Do you fancy being a copyist in the consistory? You are dear to me."

But, for some time now, Gavriil had been hoping for more— but for what?

A splendid continuation of the Name Day celebration

THE ECCLESIASTICAL GUESTS—the Rylsk archimandrite Iakinf Karpinsky, the Putivl superior Manuil Levitsky, the Bryansk superior Tikhon Zabela, the Cholp superior Antoniy Balabukha, and the Bryansk archpriest Vasiliy Konstantinov, among others, celebrated their archimandrite's Name Day for another few days.

They lost their image and their likeness to such an extent that they became truly spiritual figures. Some of them developed fits, which were common following such labors, and were taken home.

The Bryansk superior Tikhon Zabela held up bravely in the ranks headed by Kirill Fliorinsky. The dropsy to which he was prone was thus aggravated and, four months later, it was reported that His Reverence departed for the immortal kingdom.

The archpriest Vasiliy Konstantinov drank until he was delirious and, in his stupor, ran into the Bishop's stable. There, on the hay, already rested one of the younger guests, the priest Sokolov.

In his horror, Sokolov sobered up and began to read prayers over the archpriest to exorcise the devil that had taken root in the wretched. But the archpriest was softly moaning and shrieking:

"Divine archpastor, have mercy, I will never drink again!"

After washing his face, the Reverend Sokolov appeared accordingly before the Bishop and, standing before him, clasped his hands, rolled his eyes under his forehead and uttered:

"Your Grace, our archpriest is dying. This is to what sciences reduce a man! The Father Superior of Bryansk, who couldn't understand the wise conversations at the table, has gone mad and is talking nonsense, ostensibly raving."

Fliorinsky was sitting calmly and finishing his spiced wine, showing no signs of madness. He called Gavriil over and said:

"Go with the physician and have a look at this fool."

The archpriest was standing in the stall before the horse stalls. His long hair was tangled and hung over his face. His face was swollen. His lips were the color of dark cherry.

"Father," said the physician, "show me your tongue."

The cherry-colored lips parted and the archpriest said quickly and plaintively:

"No, no, gentlemen monks, you won't succeed at getting me drunk!"

The Bishop had a sister, much about whom will be said further on in this festive tale. She lived on her brother's allowance. The ill man was brought to her.

The archpriest lay on a coarse, faux-redwood ottoman with his teeth clenched and his lips presently drooping.

The physician wished to pour a cooling medicine into his mouth.

The archpriest moaned without parting his lips:

"Wine, wine, wine!"

The physician, Pavel Ivanovich Vints, who had received ecclesiastical training in these kinds of illnesses, was experienced, and replied:

"This isn't wine, but medicine I am giving you in conformity with theoretical and practical medical science to prevent you from developing *obliteruction* of the *alva* and internal gangrene."

The archpriest sobbed quietly.

The doctor inserted a knife in his teeth and continued his speech:

"This remedy is used prior to bloodletting and *visicatorias*, for, at present, your clogged nerves are not receiving proper blood circulation, which is why your pulse is irregular."

Gavriil was smiling and thinking that, just like Gil Blas de

Santillane, he had now become a doctor's aide.

"Young man," said the doctor, having finally pried the archpriest's mouth open, "take His Holiness's tongue with your hand and pull it to the side."

After this was done, medicine was poured into the archpriest's mouth in the same way horse doctors do to horses.

The next day, the archpriest recovered—or, rather, settled down and drove off to his residence.

The Bishop's chambers were cleaned, washed, and scrubbed. A thurible with laudanum was passed through the rooms.

And it was as if the air became ordinary again.

On the third morning, Vasilyev awoke and, noticing his swollen cheek, reconstructed the memory of the slap through inquiries and deduction. A complaint was brought to the Bishop.

Despite being accustomed to wine, the bishop was languorous and irritable after his Name Day celebration.

He scolded Gavriil in three dialects and, in the end, bade Gavriil to pay the cell attendant Vasilyev a ruble for disgracing him, which settled the matter.

The Adventures of Praskovya Friday

DURING THE REIGN of Catherine II, icons drawn on wood were considered worthy of worship, contrary to popular belief during the time of Peter III.

But statues carved out of wood were considered heretical, especially if they were completely round and not bas-relief.

They resembled idols.

In March, the Bishop traveled across Kromy to Oryol to restore propriety.

Kromy was a quiet town of smallholders, or free people who did not own any serfs.

These landowners were the descendants of boyars who once settled in Kromy when the town was part of the defense line against the Tatars.

Smallholders differed little from peasants in their way of life. For the most part, residents of the town of Kromy practiced farming.

As soon as His Grace walked into the Conciliar Church, his eyes fell on a tall, wood-carved statue.

"Who is she?" the Bishop asked.

"St. Friday," the priest answered.

The Bishop ordered his retinue to cover Friday with burlap and lock her away under a bell tower.

The townspeople cried bitterly for Friday and predicted various misfortunes for the bishop and his retinue. And indeed, when they traveled from Kromy to Oryol, the Deacon Maximov, who had sewn St. Friday into burlap, died.

When Kromy residents learned of this event, they were overjoyed.

Oryol welcomed the archpriest with the ringing of bells.

Before every church stood priests in robes, deacons in sticharions holding thuribles, and clerks and acolytes carrying holy water in cups and candles. People were standing in the streets, hanging off fences and sitting on straw roofs.

People were shouting, bells were ringing. Dobrynin was thinking:

"If we collect ten kopecks from everyone . . . it's good to be an arch-flamen."

The Epiphany Cathedral, where the Bishop was to hold the service, was as crowded with people as the ships sent from Riga to England are crammed with folded masts.

The next day, bread loaves, sugar, tea, coffee, lemons, fish, and other foodstuffs were brought to the Bishop's apartment.

A new life began, unclouded by anything.

The Bishop's frequent services and frequent consecrations of priests resulted in a high income for his entourage.

Frequent dinners at civilians' homes and soirées with choirboys till the break of dawn.

It seemed like the archpriest celebrated his birthday for a whole month.

Moreover, the archpriest received revenue from an opportunely trained, so-called fold of clergy and acolytes.

The town of Oryol stands where the Orlik River enters the Oka River.

The Oka's water level is low, and when goods flow from the Svensk fair, barges often run aground.

The Oka originates seventy versts away from the city, close to a village called Ochki or Oki, from which it also derives its name.

The Bragging Windmill, which belongs to Count Golovkin, overlooks the city. When they have to bring a ship ashore, they sell water from this windmill by the peaks and it serves as a floodgate.

Thus, even the water was sold in Oryol.

And men of commerce are devoted to religion.

But the archpriest couldn't appreciate his good fortune and began to expose the separatists.

At the time, devotees of the olden rites were known as separatists.

For the most part, these separatists belonged to the merchant class and many of them were wealthy.

His Grace would give anti-separatist speeches at the cathedral.

In his virulent speeches, he called separatists sons of bitches, spat at them, and babbled until he began to reminisce about Paris and swear in church.

The Bishop was informed by a priest from the Archangel church who was seeking the post of archpriest that the merchant Ovchinnikov accused him of babbling and being mad as a hatter. Furthermore, it turned out that Ovchinnikov was not saying this allegorically, but historically.

The Bishop demanded that Ovchinnikov be seized as a blasphemer.

But Ovchinnikov managed a large cattle trade and didn't wait around to be seized, having gone away on business somewhere.

The Bishop sent a denunciation to the Synod claiming that the faith, the law, the rank, and the office had suffered damages. But Ovchinnikov and his friends diverted the denunciation through their merchant offices in St. Petersburg and the Bishop received no answer to his complaint.

Moreover, in spite of the Bishop's wishes, the priest from the Archangel church couldn't obtain the title of archpriest in return for the calumny.

Dobrynin participated only circumstantially in these matters because they were not very lucrative.

Dobrynin preferred to wander down the broad, dreary streets of the town of Oryol.

Wherever Dobrynin went he was always followed by a crowd of supplicants, much like dogs follow a butcher's cart.

The crowd tenaciously followed Dobrynin, putting forth their requests. The sensible ones combined those requests with precise donation amounts.

The mad ones only wept and said:

"We are poor, we are spent, our elderly and little ones are waiting for us at home."

Dobrynin heeded the sensible ones closely, sincerely, and with priestly candor, assured them that he'd carry out their requests, set timelines, and didn't break his word.

Dobrynin didn't drive the mad to despair, but said a few totally incomprehensible words to them.

Gradually, with time, the mad ones became sensible and generous too.

Dobrynin lived as he could and worked ably.

He had a great deal of work, worked nights, and acquired the habit, when he had written a page, to fall asleep then and there, with his head on the table, waiting for the ink to dry. There would have been no need to wait if he had spread sand over it, but the letters wouldn't have come out as brilliant.

Thus, Dobrynin took turns writing and taking one-minute naps throughout the night.

Thus, a seal dozes on a northern glacier, waking up every minute and trembling before the phantom rustling of a wide-awake polar bear.

One time, sleep gripped Dobrynin by his coiffed hair and the poor seal overslept by a few minutes.

The candle melted, fell, burned his fingers, and set the papers on fire.

Dobrynin leapt to his feet and began to extinguish the fire with a fury greater than that of firemen extinguishing city fires.

The room grew dark. Dobrynin made fire by rubbing two sticks together, blew up a flame, and lit a new candle.

"Woe is me," he said. "The corners on one of the dossiers burned off."

Dobrynin began to level the burned-off corner with his scissors.

Darkness and fatigue had muddled his brain, he was seeing spots and, suddenly, he saw that he had cut off the Bishop's signature and note with his scissors.

Dobrynin sat in despair.

He remembered all analogous historical events, remembered that von Biron himself, the Duke of Courland, had the strange habit of chewing parchment. This was when von Biron still served as a copyist. And so it once happened that he chewed up and swallowed an important document.

"Von Biron didn't perish," Dobrynin thought. "Perhaps, fortune has reserved some sort of happiness for me as it did for Gil Blas, perhaps, I will be a nobleman, too."

And, saying such things to himself, he discreetly glued the Bishop's signature to the document.

And you will find out what came of this in the next chapter of this exceedingly truthful, albeit unheroic tale.

Chapter containing a description of Dobrynin's craftiness and imparting the misfortunes that befell him

HE NEEDED TO get the resolution off his hands. It was most convenient to do this later in the day, when the setting sun shone weakly through the dim glass of the archimandrite's chambers and the expensive candles weren't yet lit.

Dobrynin combed his hair better than usual, powdered it, put on brogues with shiny buckles and went to see the Bishop.

Meanwhile, the Bishop's coach rolled down the streets of Oryol.

The Bishop was sitting haughtily next to Mr. Astafyev.

The coach, which was suspended on leather straps for comfort, was pulled by eight horses.

Goats and tattered garrison soldiers flashed behind the coach windows and, suddenly, the Bishop saw Dobrynin's slender figure.

Knocking on the front glass with his finger, the Bishop stopped the coach. He graciously invited Dobrynin inside the coach.

The prophet Elijah, who was carried on a chariot to heaven, most likely didn't feel as glorified as Gavriil, whom the Bishop invited inside the coach in full view of the baker and a peasant woman selling pumpkin seeds.

The coach began to rattle.

The Bishop glanced at the chief commissioner and said, pointing to Dobrynin:

"He is my most reliable one."

Then, taking Dobrynin by the hand that wasn't holding documents, he said:

"Continue as you have begun."

Dobrynin raised his eyes to the sky.

The coach's sky was draped with light-blue quilted silk embellished with flower bouquets.

Dobrynin served the documents in the Bishop's chambers along with the town news; the candles weren't yet lit and the glued-on piece went unnoticed.

Thus, Dobrynin ascended.

Gavriil had already become accustomed to having money in his pocket and ordered himself a silk double wallet with rings. Silver rather than copper wire was conspicuously strung through the silk loops.

But then, the persecution began.

For unknown reasons, the Bishop's sister hated Dobrynin.

At one time, she had been married off to the cathedral key-keeper, but the key-keeper mixed up directions; rather than carry parcels to the Bishop's bedchamber, he carried them out of it. Hence, he was probed with sticks in that very bedchamber and then sent to the Kiev monastery, where he met his end.

The Bishop's sister was left a widow with two daughters. And, supposedly, she had a rivalry with Dobrynin.

They departed Oryol to the sound of ringing bells, but now, not only weren't there people sitting on fences, but also none in the streets.

Because Oryol residents were fed up with His Grace, so to speak.

They came to Sevsk and here word spread that Dobrynin allegedly removed close to one thousand rubles from Oryol, which was intolerable.

The Bishop himself began to say that he would get his hands on Dobrynin.

On the festive day of the episcopal service, Kirill marched in a procession from the empyrean seat to his pulpit.

An empyrean seat is a special gilded and carved balcony with bas-relief, but not round, angels made of wood. Here, the humble bishops preside.

After sitting on the empyrean seat, the Bishop deigned to go to the altar. It must be said, judicious reader, that deacons aren't allowed to sit at an altar, while a woman, by the way, like a dog, may not be present at an altar at all.

But a cat may.

A priest may even sit at an altar.

The Bishop had an armchair at the altar, which was known as a pulpit.

The Bishop sat down in the armchair and was supposed to listen to Dobrynin recite the Eucharistic prayers for the communion on his behalf; but hardly did Dobrynin begin to read in his velvet voice, which was already not a soprano, but an alto, when he felt two hands sink into his hair.

Fliorinsky was a strong man, and his hands didn't at all look as soft as down.

He dragged Gavriil around by the hair at the altar in the same way a falcon drags a hen around.

Dust had risen at the altar.

The first kick intended for Dobrynin landed on the throne.

The throne began to hum.

Then, the archimandrite Karpinsky got his due—he had prudently jumped up on the windowsill.

The acolytes scattered around different corners of the altar, awaiting the end of His Grace's assault with reverence and fear. Concert singing continued in the church. And the Bishop beat Gavriil's head and neck in time to it.

Finally, his fury subsided. The Bishop was out of breath.

"Where did I fail, Your Grace?" Dobrynin uttered in a pitiful voice.

It turned out that the Bishop's hassock wasn't placed before his podium. A hassock is a small round rug with an eagle embroidered on it.

The Bishop didn't observe this oversight himself—it was pointed out to him by the righteous archimandrite.

A hassock was served and the Bishop sat down.

In the heat of the moment, Dobrynin began to tear up the Eucharistic prayers.

Fliorinsky sat eating the wafer and washing it down with Kagor wine, while Dobrynin rattled on:

"May His Grace's Eucharist bring joy, health, and merriment, may he, during the terrible second coming, be considered worthy of admission at the right hand of God . . ."

When he returned to his chamber, Dobrynin definitively lost heart. His body hurt, his soul hurt. Dobrynin's entourage consisted of a few acolytes and choirboys, and he was humiliated before his entire entourage.

At night, Dobrynin couldn't sleep.

It seemed to him that the Bachelor of Salamanca came to his cell in real life wearing a feathered hat and a silk suit; then the Bishop arrived in a coach drawn by sturgeons and here, in this very room, began to perform his service, singeing Gavriil's face. As for Gavriil, he was no longer Dobrynin, but Don Cherubim de la Ronda, but he stole that title somewhere and glued it on. Whereas the Bishop arrived on sturgeons and began tearing beards and singeing his face with candles and kicking and talking about Paris. And the Bishop's face! . . . Why did the Bishop Fliorinsky look so familiar? Maybe, it wasn't the Bishop, but de la Ronda? And this, apparently, isn't de la Ronda, but the physician Vints.

At this moment, his fever rose, darkness fell, and I herewith end the chapter.

Chapter containing something of a mystery

IN THE MORNING, the Bishop visited the ill one himself.

He somberly felt for Gavriil's pulse, looked at his tongue.

The flushed and frenzied Dobrynin lay there not recognizing anyone.

The Bishop went out, closed the door, and stood there.

The cell attendant stood in silence before him.

"Go," Kirill said in a hollow voice, "go tell him," he continued louder, "that I don't hold any anger toward him."

Dobrynin lay there unconscious. The fever streamed about him like water. Suddenly, he heard a voice.

It was the cell attendant screaming in his ear.

"His Grace doesn't have a grudge against you."

"He doesn't?" Dobrynin asked. "Alright, I will get up! Are there any clerks in the bureau?"

His face reddened, Dobrynin got up, went to the bureau, began to write, was overcome by a chill and fell face-first on a document, imprinting on his cheek the names of the men accepted to the holy order.

The choirboy Kozma Vysheslavtsev, who played the gusli—a merry drunkard, but kind—picked up Dobrynin and carried him to the bed of Gedeon the sacristan—at that moment, Dobrynin couldn't be carried very far. He lay there dreaming of gilded Parisian bells and the Bishop's canes.

And who's this? It appears that his mother came?

He had forgotten her and she came as a nun.

"You're a nun, mother, why are you crying? There is nothing wrong with being a nun.

"But why are you crying? And why is His Grace nearby?

"Your Grace, why are you crying? Your Grace, don't you recall?"

"Absalom, my son," His Grace uttered.

"Yes, I recall, Your Grace, I read about it. Absalom rebelled against his father, David, and Absalom's hair was long, and Absalom's hair got tangled up in the branches. And the mule rode out from under the prince and Absalom was hung by his hair. Absalom died and David cried: 'Oh Absalom, my son . . .'"

And here's what Vints said:

"We need to conduct a purge to clean his entrails. Don't be dismayed, Your Grace, the young man isn't ill because you dragged him by the hair. This is a harmful fever with spots, typhus."

Vints left.

"Mother, why are you crying on His Grace's shoulder? Why do you reproach him? After all, I'm not his son, but the son of a Rodogozh priest. It doesn't make any sense. Kiev, the tilted hat of the monastery on the mountain. The Dnieper River rising azure and hot."

The morning spread out on His Grace's quilted blanket in patches of sunlight.

Dobrynin awoke and was surprised.

Upon him lay His Grace's blanket—a great favor.

He wanted to eat.

Kozma Vysheslavtsev sat before him and asked:

"Have you recovered, boy?"

Vints, the ordinary Vints, came in the room and said:

"The fever has broken, I will ask them to prepare you barley with chicken."

Then, a gentle eighty-year-old man named Paley came.

He patted Dobrynin's hands and said:

"Sins, my son. The Bishop asked about you a lot, came to see you."

"And where is my mother?" Gavriil asked.

Paley grew a bit confused and said:

"Yes, your mother was here, but now she has returned to the convent . . . Well, feel better."

Gavriil had a difficult recovery; his weakness prevented him from standing up on his feet.

He asked about the Bishop.

It turned out that the Bishop left for the funeral of His Grace Kirill Lyashevetsky of Chernigov.

The latter had burned to death while reading in bed.

The wax candle melted and fell, lighting his brocade dressing gown on fire.

It was as if the Bishop used this as a pretext to go away and came back as if nothing happened, but, from this day forward, Gavriil began to call him uncle in private.

New dignity

ONE TIME, IN August, Dobrynin entered the Bishop's chambers. He called the young man over to the canapé on which he lay.

He began, as was his habit, with a text from the Holy Scripture:

"Bow down thine ear; and forget your people and your father's home, and may the king desire thy goodness."

Having uttered the words of the Prophet and King David, the Bishop continued in prose, so to speak:

"For a while, my intention has been to make you closer to me. Your diligence and meticulousness in all your duties have for a while incited me to distinguish you from the rest of the household."

Dobrynin was pleased, and the Bishop continued in the same languorous voice:

"Starting today, you shall be my cell attendant instead of Vasilyev, who was dismissed for drunkenness."

Dobrynin wasn't expecting this. He stood there like a pillar of salt.

He knew that, in the past three years, nine cell attendants fled from His Grace's clutches, and thus began to apologize and decline incoherently.

But the Bishop continued tenderly:

"Are you concerned that those nine left so ignominiously? It couldn't have been otherwise, since none of them had your intelligence, loyalty, or decorum. A man who doesn't have all three qualities at once isn't fit for any noble position."

Then, sighing and without his usual bitterness, the Bishop continued serenely:

"My intention is higher and nobler than you may think. My intention is to differ from you in name and position only and to share a soul with you."

These words touched Dobrynin with the sinister promise contained in them. And he threw himself at His Grace's feet in deep silence.

This is, generally, standard conduct within the confines of the monastery.

Lifting up his new cell attendant, His Grace showed him the wardrobe, the cupboard, and, once more, the silverware.

His Grace's soul was uneasy.

Narrow is the monastery, high is the monastery wall, and Fliorinsky ran in it like a squirrel in a barbed-wire wheel. Only not over twigs, but over people.

As a result of his melancholy, Kirill Fliorinsky grew to love menial labor—firing bricks and lime and chopping wood—and thus developed the habit of waking up at dawn and bringing his entire cell staff along—the attendant, the choirboy, two coal heavers, guards, and lumberjacks.

Only Dobrynin remained at home.

And so he had to, first, clean the table knives, candlesticks, and basins, then, take up the brush, and then, the broom, changing up the order for variety's sake.

Thus he worked, singing a ditty to himself about presently sharing a soul with the Bishop.

It wasn't what Dobrynin expected, having left the post of a man of the quill. But an even worse future was in store for him.

It seemed that the Bishop was keeping him close and, at the same time, hated him as someone who knew a certain secret.

One time, Gavriil was sitting on the floor in deep dejection and counting the Bishop's dirty linen when the furious hierarch suddenly ran in and deafened him with the question:

"Were you in church today?"

"I was," Dobrynin answered quickly.

"And what was the gospel we read today?"

Dobrynin was silent. The pontiff, having seized his Absalom hair, uttered:

"In church, we read the gospel, 'Wherever I am, there my servant shall be.' And you're not with me all day, particularly when I need you, when I'm carrying wood chips out of the newly-built church."

Dobrynin ran to the church and cleared wood chips and various litter; in the evening, he was reprimanded for neglecting domestic tasks, while, at night, he counted the Bishop's dirty linen.

In the morning, he was ordered to serve tea, but the Bishop didn't drink the tea and ran off to level the ground for the new bell tower.

And he had to serve the tea there, where the Bishop ordered that Dobrynin lug soil around on a barrow. Moreover, he bitterly reproached Gavriil for losing his hair.

"Your hair," he said, "was like Absalom's. Why don't you have your hair anymore?"

"Owing to fever and labor," Dobrynin replied.

New moon

RUMORS RAN THAT the Bishop wasn't in his right mind, that, when the moon rose, he wandered around the monastery with his eyes closed in a somnambulistic state.

A new moon was approaching and the Bishop was becoming

increasingly irritable; Dobrynin couldn't think about anything anymore.

One time, at night, he heard from the glass cupboard, through the unclosed glass doors, that someone was speaking in the sitting room. Dobrynin got up.

The moon shone over the sitting room, the Bishop wandered around in the dark and only the lower half of his body was illuminated.

The Bishop spoke affectedly, then rapidly, then shrieked:

"I am the Prince-Bishop and not some sort of peasant in bast shoes like the other Russian bishops. Come hear what the Sevsk Bishop has to say.

"Potemkin—wasn't he a deacon's pupil? Didn't he plan to join the holy order, didn't I surpass him in rhetorical debates?

"And where has the one-eyed one ascended to now?

"And I get a hassock with an eagle under my feet. But am I a bird myself?"

And the Bishop muttered about bears, elks, elephants, and cows, languished, and talked about the singing, howling, invoking, and jabbering beasts.

Then, he began to laugh softly.

"Yes, you are dead, my Chernigov friend. Your dressing gown was fastened on four hooks and burned, you couldn't have torn it off. And I could never tear off my habit."

At first, Dobrynin was sad, then he grew bored. He stepped back, closed the glass door and lay down in the cupboard again, putting the Bishop's dirty linen under his head in place of a pillow.

And the Bishop continued to mutter there, in the sitting room.

Dobrynin wanted only one thing—to sleep.

To sleep for twelve hours without interruption.

In the morning, His Grace called him very early.

The cell attendant came up to him in the dark to take his orders.

Without opening his eyes, the Bishop said:

"Do you wish to get married?"

"No," Gavriil answered.

"You will!" the Bishop said. "I have a bride for you, she lives with my sister, she is my ward, marry her."

"I don't want to," Gavriil responded.

"Why ever not?"

"It is too early for me to get married."

"Alright, go forth." The Bishop ended his dark audience.

Dobrynin knew this stout girl, the Bishop's ward.

She was twenty-five and lived with the Bishop's sister.

It was an unprofitable business.

Dobrynin thought it was almost as if he was the Bishop's ward and the Bishop wished to be rid of two wards at once.

During the day, Kirill was incensed. At dinner, he threw an apple at Dobrynin with such force that the armchairs rolled back an arshin.

In the evening, the Bishop sat on his bed in the bedchamber and trimmed the hair of a small dog, speaking to it affectionately in French.

Dobrynin walked in and took a monastic bow, uttering:

"I humbly ask Your Grace to dismiss me from my current position and assign me to my previous one."

The Bishop threw the scissors on the blanket and turned up his nose. The half-trimmed dog jumped on the floor, yapping.

"Skeptic," uttered the Bishop, "why do you disbelieve?"

Then, after a few more seconds of silence, the Bishop leapt up from under his blanket and ran to the pantry.

Dobrynin kept quiet in his confusion.

Suddenly, a red fox fur flew out of the dark pantry, then another, then a third—and this continued until there were eighteen.

After the foxes came the Bishop himself.

"Here, take," he said, "sew yourself a fur coat. You can buy your own fabric for the lining."

After a few seconds of silence, he added:

"You have the money."

Thus, this fur coat, which was like a peace offering, was assembled, and any talk of matchmaking died down for some time.

Plots and têtes-à-têtes, denunciations, and other monastery matters

THE BISHOP'S CHAMBERS were often visited by the consistory member Irinarch Rudanovsky and the Latin teacher Sadovsky. Together with Dobrynin, they formed a single outfit.

Sadorsky called Rudanovsky his father and Dobrynin his brother and friend.

Thus, they were like a holy family.

Sadorsky was an experienced and offhandedly honey-tongued man.

It must be said that, traditionally, a bishop doesn't have the right to file a petition to be transferred to another episcopate.

The Holy Synod may transfer him of its own accord, so to speak.

Thus, bishops petition for it in roundabout ways.

All the Sevsk residents were waiting for the Bishop Fliorinsky to finally leave.

At this time, Dobrynin showed Rudanovsky a letter that he stole from His Grace.

The letter was a reply from the Chief Secretary of the Synod Ostolopov. Evidently, the Bishop had requested a transfer because Ostolopov wrote the following:

"While I am a true friend to Your Grace, my current position at the Synod does not entitle me to hold forth on your transfer, and I dare not assure you that it will in the future."

Having read this letter, Rudanovsky sent a request to the Synod to be transferred to a Malorussian monastery.

Rudanovsky's brother was in the Synod and a transfer followed.

Now, Sadorsky was left with Dobrynin.

Dobrynin thought they would play a duet, but Sadorsky decided to play a solo.

One time, the Bishop returned from the grove looking glum.

Spies reported to Dobrynin that Sadorsky had a tête-à-tête with the Bishop. The Bishop sat down in his armchair, rubbed his beard with his hands, and asked with vexation and consternation:

"What kinds of discussions did you have with Irinarch about me?"

"The usual ones," Dobrynin answered.

"And the letter," the Bishop declared, "which letter did you show Irinarch?"

The attack was not unexpected.

Dobrynin was raised in a monastery and was accustomed to maintaining a secret friendship with even a rat if it had access to some ascetic and could report something about him. Thus, he replied firmly and sweetly:

"I had no qualms about showing the letter because there was no secret in it, and we read it deploring that other undeserving Bishops are receiving transfers, while Your Grace, who is so renowned for their education, is not being sufficiently rewarded."

"No, ungrateful one," the Bishop said, "you can't deceive me. Admit to everything, this will alleviate your lot."

He had to confess, at least about Sadorsky—such was the monastery rule—and, moreover, he had to, so to say, go on the offensive.

Dobrynin exclaimed:

"I will report everything I can remember! I only ask for your patience in listening to me."

"Everyone out!" cried the spirited Bishop.

"When, in our talks," Dobrynin continued, "we came upon the subject of Your Grace, Sadorsky and I agreed that you are hurtful to people who are loyal to you. You scold them at every turn and give free rein to your hands even in public, which is why anyone genuinely subservient to you loses their sense of loyalty. Thus, we wholeheartedly wished for Your Grace to receive a higher-level bishopric so that your heart would, so to say, soften, and we could have peace."

"Bah!" cried the Bishop. "And who taught you such eloquence? What about patience?" he barked even louder.

Then, in accordance with monastery tradition, Dobrynin threw himself at the Bishop's feet and cried:

"I told the whole truth and Sadorsky will confirm it."

"And how would he know?" asked the Bishop slyly, growing red.

"He," Dobrynin answered, "advised me to steal your letter and gathered evidence about you that was close at hand; it was also he who confused Your Grace's soul with regard to me."

"No," the Bishop retorted, "he is a noble man and I will destroy you before I destroy him."

Under the pretense of visiting the Kiev metropolitan, His Grace called on Irinarch Rudanovsky, whom Dobrynin had the chance to inform about everything.

Irinarch's account did not diverge from Dobrynin's. And the Bishop confirmed his suspicion that his main enemy was Sadorsky.

Kiev grew duller during this visit.

Dobrynin visited the famous lavra and went into the seminary.

Many rural and out-of-town fathers wished to have their sons educated, but could not provide for them owing to poverty.

Thanks to contributions from generous citizens and the help

of monasteries, every seminary had a spacious izba with an oven or two. The monastery supplied these izbas with fuel and nothing else.

These were adobe izbas, which is to say they were made of wicker dabbed with yellow clay on the inside and outside and left unbleached.

The roofs were made of straw. The windows were round.

Here, the seminary subsisted on alms and theft.

Having inspected this establishment, Dobrynin decided that even a bishop's assistant's life was easier.

But the seminarians' life was considered wicked by the State as well.

The Ukrainian seminary differed from the Great Russian one.

The Great Russian one consisted of priests' sons and lacked any significance, so to say. As for the Ukrainian, the Kiev one, it was composed of men of various origins. Here, the Ukrainian nobility was educated and brought together, and its graduates continued on not only to monasteries.

Thus, the spotlight had been turned on the Kiev seminary. And the new Kiev Metropolitan Gavriil Kremenetsky was in charge of Russification.

In two years' time, the wooden unrestricted seminary was destroyed and the one-story seminary was built from stone.

But only priests' sons were admitted to it.

The Metropolitan said it was necessary to sever the tie between the clergy and Malorussian citizenry and confine the former within the limits of a clerical order.

Gavriil was hospitable because there was an old Ukrainian tradition, undisputed by him, that, on the Metropolitan's birthday and Christmas Day, he was brought silk, sugar, white bread, lemons, and sugarloaves.

Only on New Year's Eve could one be admitted to see Gavriil without an offering.

This was the opening that the Sevsk bishop was aiming for, but this opening was fully filled.

Fliorinsky managed only to dine at Gavriil Kremenetsky's table.

The latter conducted himself simply over dinner and bragged about his common origins.

Gavriil Kremenetsky was the son of the prefect of the town of Nosovka in the Kiev regiment. According to the State, this was supposed to mitigate Ukrainians' bitterness. He ate cured roach at the table and repeated:

"My mother brought me up on this fish."

Then, as he was still talking, the Kiev Bishop pushed aside the plate with the torn fish tails and heads and said:

"I lived in St. Petersburg for a long time and became used to their rituals and customs. Now I don't know; should I be the one to follow Malorussian customs or should Malorussians adapt to my Petersburg ways?"

The holy Kiev Metropolitan's entire entourage at the table stood up piously and reverently, and answered in unison that all of Kiev must take His Holiness as an example.

After a brief silence, our Prince-Bishop, too, had to stand up.

Seeing that the performance was over and that both smoked fish and Petersburg ways were politically effective here, Kirill Fliorinsky said:

"Your Grace, you have earned from the homeland the right not to change yourself in any way."

With that, the performance was over.

Kirill returned to tiny Sevsk with a gloomy face.

Again, they pressed forward with the inquiry. It turned out that Sadorsky himself spied on the Bishop through the choirboys, who kept sentry at the eparch's.

Sadorsky taught the choirboys Latin, so they were under his thumb, so to speak.

Sadorsky was invited to the table. At the table, the Bishop

spoke of various matters, furiously boring the earth and all that dwelled on it, but not revealing the target of his fury.

As he spoke, the Bishop grabbed a carafe of water and threw it against the floor. Droplets of water rose in the room like a fog.

Sadorsky trembled in his chair.

"Oh, you're trembling!" the Bishop exclaimed. "Therefore, your conscience is not clear. You vagabond, get out of the hall! Servants, chase him out with brooms!"

Sadorsky was ousted, but the next day, it was announced that, when he departed, he stole from the wall the Bishop's handwritten instructions and schedule of rates for consecration.

Sadorsky instructed the sacristan Zakharov to do it.

In a fit of anger, the Bishop ordered his retinue to place Zakharov in chains and have him drafted into the army.

This was done too hastily.

During the Christmas fast, an order arrived from the Senate and the Synod to return the sacristan from military service and explain to the Synod: first, why did the Bishop hang a handwritten schedule of rates in contravention of the ordinance forbidding the collecting of money for consecration, and second, why did the Bishop collect bribes at all?

It turned out that Sadorsky joined forces with the Oryol merchants—Old Believers, who were fed up with the Bishop's yelling.

Despondency and sadness showed on the Bishop's face as he summoned the principal informers: one from the Belgorodsk province and the other from the Orlovsk one.

The informers deliberated with him and decided that things looked bleak because the adversary was crafty and rich and that, furthermore, he could have collected more than double those sums, but he shouldn't have hung a handwritten schedule of rates on the wall.

The Svensky monastery, also known as the Swinesky monastery, and its environs

THE SVENSKY MONASTERY—also known as the Uspensky monastery and the Novo-Pechersky monastery—is subject to the Kiev-Pechersky Lavra.

The populace had, without any rancor, nicknamed this monastery the Swinesky, although it sits on a river called the Sven.

The Swinesky monastery was renowned for its large fairs, which took place on monastery grounds and generated significant profits.

The monastery was enormous and built entirely from stone; the bell tower and cathedral were built according to Rastrelli's 1758 plan.

The monastery superior was a man endowed with both spiritual and social graces. His name was Father Palladiy, his hair was black, his eyes shone as if they were lacquered, and his voice was clear.

And he could joke well with noblemen and noblewomen alike.

The Father Superior had an especially agreeable time in September, when, for four weeks, a crowded fair bustled before the monastery walls.

Kirill Fliorinsky also bustled here, but behind the walls.

Thence, he'd go off to visit other monasteries and to dine with the most distinguished landowners; and thence he drove out to the estate of the gentleman Thaddeus Tyutchev.

Tyutchev's wooden house had not been decorated by a miserly hand.

Brocade wallpaper and paintings, cabinets and armoires, tables and redwood bureaus.

Servants in liveries called "lackeys." The valet wore silk.

Fifty persons of both sexes sat at the table and the host

presided over it, albeit in a dressing gown and nightcap.

Holy sky, you alone know how much English beer, wine, and punch was spilt or, more accurately, consumed here.

The feast began at the exact moment of the guests' arrival in the evening and continued in the garden.

The weather was just marvelous, though golden September had already removed the beautiful garments from most trees and swathed the ground in them.

The host was the first to be smitten; he was carried from the garden to the bedchamber, deprived of all sight, hearing, smell, and feeling.

The hierarch stayed in his seat and yelled at the host's servants:

"Your master committed a fatal sin when he prematurely jumped ship against all regulations, and, for that, he shall be handed over to the clerical court!"

In an attempt to extinguish the troubles, Father Superior Palladiy and the Bryansk archpriest shouted to the servants to roll out new barrels of wine from the cellar.

In the garden, two thousand candles were lit in bowls and the sky turned rosy.

At ten in the morning, His Grace deigned to go to bed and the host deigned to awaken.

Time was passing, September was ending and the fair was dispersing, as were the emptied fair wagons; the last birds had flown to the south; having gorged on the harvest, the quails hopped and soared, heading south.

The Bishop's heavily loaded carts were leaving for Sevsk.

He was seen off for a while and his horses were harnessed and unharnessed a few times.

They drove out at night.

The bells rang and, all in all, this resembled a night terror rather than a ceremony.

The gentleman Major Bakhtin accompanied the Bishop's cart.

Behind him, Dobrynin rode on the Major's horse, leading

both the Bishop's and Bakhtin's choirboys.

The Bishop's choirboys were dressed in Polish caftans with long sleeves thrown behind their backs.

Bakhtin's choirboys were dressed as dragoons.

They sang merry songs together.

My dear lady
Varvarushka
Don't be offended
That I haven't called on you . . .

And in the first carriage, the Bishop sang along and Father Palladiy produced sweet-sounding roulades, his lacquered eyes twinkling in the dark.

Sticking his head out of the carriage, Mr. Bakhtin yelled:

"The horse, the saddle, and the pistols are yours!"

It was nothing new for Dobrynin to accept gifts.

And he saluted Bakhtin with his hat in time to the song.

During their overnight stop, Palladiy impersonated Pechersky cathedral elders, village priests, coachmen, and seminarians in ludicrous and candid situations.

Such was the month of September.

Such was the Bishop's harvest.

I regret that I must note, however, that, in the winter, Bakhtin demanded payment for the gifts and received a sum of money, albeit an insignificant one.

The stripped Wonder-worker and Mr. Kasagov

No, Mr. Bakhtin was not a real nobleman.

It would be more accurate to say that he was issued from the Smolensk szlachta.

On the other hand, Yelisey Khitrov, the military commander

of Karachev, did come from real nobility.

He received the guests in the former St. Tikhon monastery.

In any case, the military commander was already retired.

They all drank together—the Bishop indicted by the court, the military chief discharged by the court, and the well-to-do Father Superior Palladiy.

Palladiy poured wine into an expensive crystal glass and appeared to ponder whether he, Palladiy, had capacity for this wine.

Whereupon Khitrov remarked:

"Father Palladiy, what if we throw in the former monastery villages with this wine?"

"Yes," Father Palladiy replied, "what if we throw in the former Karachev military chancery with this wine?"

And the entire civilian and holy rank roared with laughter.

Again, they rode out at night with torches and fanfare.

They spent the night at the Odrino-Nikolayevsky monastery.

Here, upon touring the church, the Bishop found a carved icon of St. Nicholas, the Wonder-worker from Myra.

The icon was carved rather than painted and bas-relief rather than round, which meant it both fit and didn't fit the criteria for the ban.

The icon was a half-arshin long.

The icon was masterfully spangled with pearls of various sizes. The robe, the hassock, the stole, the pallium, and the miter were embroidered with pearls.

Diamonds were inserted in the pearls in the most suitable places. Having examined this icon, the Bishop called Dobrynin over.

"Education is a glorious thing," the Bishop said. "For instance, I look at this statue and I recall Greek antiquity. Dionysus, if my memory serves me right—but I'm preaching to the choir here—ordered to remove the golden mantle off a statue of Aesculapius with the words that 'in the summer, this mantle is hot, in the winter, it is cold and may be conveniently replaced with a woolen one.' And we shall peel this Wonder-worker like an egg."

An order was given to strip the Wonder-worker and store the bare wooden carving in the church sacristy; as for the pearls and diamonds, the Bishop used them to make himself a hat, a cross, and a panagia.

The Bishop's merry band was joined by a landowner, the Captain of Artillery Ivan Sokolov, and his father, a priest—the same one who had read the exorcising prayer over the drunken Bryansk archpriest in the horse stall.

The Bishop was invited to this Sokolov's house to discuss a private matter.

Captain Sokolov was married to a noblewoman, née Kasagova, while Andrey Ivanovich Kasagov, a Guard Captain, led a dissolute life and started a harem at his home.

Thus, was it possible to take away from this Andrey Ivanovich, an unreliable person in the moral sense, his estate, and, at the very least, place it under the conservatorship of his relative, the Captain's wife Kasagova?

The Bishop replied graciously:

"We shall see."

They sat down at the table and began to sing the traditional Cherubic Hymn, a Greek chant. Then, they sang seminarian songs and drank, when, all of a sudden, Sokolov's servant ran in and announced:

"Kasagov is here!"

The Bishop immediately bid everyone to take their places. He abandoned singing, went into the bedchamber, brushed his hair, sprayed on perfume, and rinsed his mouth because the stray sheep would be able to smell wine on him.

Palladiy was sent to meet Kasagov.

The Father Superior spoke about the laws on flagrant fornicators, causing the Guard Captain some embarrassment.

Then, arm in arm with the choirboys, the Bishop himself came out to meet the stray sheep.

Kasagov turned out to be a quiet man of average height and slight build.

He bore the marks of a good upbringing.

He spoke with difficulty, as if trying to recall the words.

He reverently invited His Grace to his home, to which His Grace consented, knowing that such visits burdened his wallet, and not with copper.

In the morning, they drove to Kasagov's village.

The church was made of stone, but run-down and cluttered.

The lunch table was bountiful, but disorderly.

At the table, Kasagov was served two roasted sparrows. He deigned to eat one, washed it down with wine, and was immediately drunk.

His Grace drank little and carried on a conversation suitable for a good pastor. His Grace spoke well, even using some Latin, and everyone at the table almost teared up, washing down His Grace's speech with the host's wine.

Only Kasagov was neither touched nor frightened, neither cheerful nor woeful.

Kirill was displeased and bid them to harness the horses for departure.

He was bored with this mirthless drunk.

Kasagov cheered up immediately and rushed over to the one and then the other, asking them to stay.

His Grace resisted. At that moment, the Guardsman fell to his knees and spoke:

"If Your Grace doesn't spend the night here, I will shoot myself."

"There's no need for that," His Grace said, and decided to stay.

After finishing supper, the Bishop went to bed. The host perked up and also went away somewhere.

Dobrynin went to Palladiy's room.

Here, Sokolov was sitting with his wife.

"Speak of the devil!" they greeted Gavriil.

Sokolov's wife, who was still young, took Gavriil by the hand and said:

"I have long wished to speak to you."

They sat down on the canapé together.

Sokolov said gaily:

"Be careful, young gentleman, don't make my wife lose her senses!"

Whereupon Gavriil replied gallantly:

"Don't worry, we will finish whatever is necessary on this sofa before your eyes."

At that moment, Lady Sokolov spoke up, smiling:

"My relative Kasagov is becoming unreasonable. He has gathered a half-squadron of soldiers, trained them personally, confers titles on them, promotes lackeys to chamberlains and gives them vests of various colors. This wouldn't warrant disapproval if he made use of his soldiers solely for his amusement. But he is directing them to insult his neighbors and tyrannize the helpless. He has started a harem, which consists not only of serfs. The village priest's daughter is in this harem, and rumor has it that her father has been exterminated by Kasagov because no one knows where he has gone. For now, this harem has been transferred to another village. But as soon as His Grace leaves, it will start all over again, and my heart bleeds for it."

Dobrynin still couldn't grasp the gist of this poignant conversation, and answered rather halfheartedly:

"Your reasoning, Madam, does credit to your heart. However, judging from daily spectacles, much in the world requires correction. But the world's evil may be neither corrected nor grieved."

Lady Sokolov retorted spiritedly:

"It is evident that Father Palladiy has not related to you that Mr. Kasagov is a relative of mine. We are not closely related, but I am his only heiress. If Kasagov were deemed insane, the inheritance would be transferred to us and we would most likely prevent our unfortunate relative from going down this treacherous path. Father Palladiy is already attending to this. Will you not take on the task of intimating to His Grace what you've heard from me?"

"Alright," Dobrynin answered.

At this time, Mr. Sokolov himself spoke up from the other end of the room.

"Young man," he said, "I know that he who toils ought to be fed."

In the morning, the toiling one had already reported Kasagov's antics to the Bishop, adding that the host was afflicted with concupiscence and that people should be afraid of even touching him.

And Dobrynin added another phrase that was customary of the Bishop's cell attendants.

"I don't know what to do with the fiend," said the Bishop, "should I excommunicate him from the Orthodox Church?"

But in the morning, coffee with fine hors d'oeuvres was served, then lunch, and the day turned out short.

In the evening, fireworks were set off and they drank again.

And the next morning, Kasagov demonstrated his squadron's maneuvers and rifle practice, and the Bishop even took part in commanding these exercises from a window.

Afterward, lunch was served again, and, at lunch, they incessantly fired from small cannons. Then, the host showered the Bishop with gifts and gave Dobrynin an expensive Turkish gun and a few pieces of gold.

Later on, the bells rang and the Bishop rode off, leaving Kasagov with his squadron and the priest's daughter.

In any case, four months after the Bishop left, Mr. Kasagov

died precipitously and it wasn't Sokolov who received the inheritance, but Samoylov, a relative of Kasagov. As for Sokolov, he received a buyout in the form of a title.

And we don't know what happened to the priest's daughter.

Mr. Safonov and the fleet-footed Greek, combined into a single chapter

THOSE WHO PRESENTLY travel all over the country in train cars or fly over it cannot begin to imagine the pleasures of the Bishop's journeys.

The Bishop maintained a correspondence with Second Major Safonov. Their correspondence was full of invective: Safonov wished to expel his village priest and the Bishop opposed this.

They drove up to the house in a wagon train.

The master came out in a flesh-colored dressing gown and shoes.

A small gray braid was stretched like a cord across the very temple of this venerable landowner.

The Bishop raised himself from the pillows and said in the voice of a man who was sleeping after dinner and wine and was displeased to awaken:

"Who are you?"

"I am the master of these parts," the old man replied.

"And how dare you address your parcels 'To His Grace Father Kirill,' as if you were writing to your priest? Too lazy to write out a Bishop's title?"

"Stop it, papa," Safonov answered, "you're my father, I'm your son, and I don't know any other titles."

The Bishop looked at his interlocutor and uttered wearily:

"Alright, be my son, you have my paternal blessing." And he climbed off his traveling carriage.

The host's table was spectacular.

The host's young son—a Guard Officer—sat at the table.

They drank a lot, drank to each other's health and even quarreled in French.

Then, they decided to inspect the cellar.

The cellar was quiet, cool, and dry.

The Bishop noticed that there was an icon of a saint hanging in the cellar.

"Sainthood is compromised," the Bishop uttered, "you cannot hang icons in cellars and baths."

The host was silent.

"You cannot hang icons in cellars," the Bishop said. "Suppose I order that the bottoms of all your barrels be smashed in."

Then, the host yelled:

"Don't you know that I'm the master of this house? You may have the power to tie me up in church, but I will tie you up in my own cellar!"

At first, the Bishop was dumbfounded by this, but then, having reconciled with the host, he even wished to exchange crosses with him. But, out of absentmindedness, he took the host's heavy gold cross and failed to give him his own, promising to send it along later.

And on rolled the Bishop's heavy horse wagons with undiminishing provisions—mobile cornucopias.

En route, the Bishop was welcomed at the Glukhov monastery by the Greek bishop Anatoliy Meles.

This Bishop loved to walk around barefoot wearing a nankeen dressing gown over his naked body.

When they entered the Bishop's chambers, the guests chanced upon a lovely and flushed young woman who was hurrying away.

The Greek cheerfully greeted the guests, shuffling with his bare feet.

"I'm very glad to see a friend," he said. "You're just in time! I have recovered, but, just a moment ago, was trembling with fever."

"Indeed," Kirill answered, "we've just encountered her as we entered."

After this pleasant conversation, they first dined and then wished to ring the bells, but the fleet-footed Greek said:

"I may be a monk but, having officiated on the crests of ships in the latest war against the Turks, I've become accustomed to gunpowder and the rumble of cannons and have thus ordered to remove the bells from my church and cast them into cannons."

Having spoken these words, Anatoliy Meles waved a kerchief in the window and the cannons began to roar.

Chapter containing particulars about the Greek bishop Meles that were unknown to Gavriil Dobrynin

MELES WAS NEITHER a Greek nor a bishop.

In January 1751, the Greek Bishop Anatoliy, who went by the name of Meles, arrived in Moscow, where he was summoned to the Synod Office and testified about his identity as well as the purpose of his travels. His testimony was involuntary.

The Synod official wrote down Meles's testimony:

"He is twenty-eight years of age; his father Vasiliy was born in Wallachia, in the town of Raya-Brailov, and, having departed thence many years ago, presently lives in Malorussia, in the shtetl of Zolotonosha of the Pereyaslav regiment, where he, Anatoliy, was born; as for Anatoliy's given name, it was Alexiy. When he, Anatoliy, came of age, the aforesaid father sent him to the Kiev Academy to learn Latin and other dialects, where he, Anatoliy, studied until 1743, attending poetics school; at present, he, Anatoliy, has forgotten Yiddish and German, but can speak and write in Greek and Latin. In 1743, with the permission of his abovementioned father, he, Anatoliy, traveled to the aforesaid Wallachian town of Raya-Brailov. After arriving in this town, he lived with his relatives for a month-and-a-half and, upon learning from them that there was a holy monastery in the vicinity of that town called Tristen, went to that monastery and lived there for four months."

In simpler terms and without equivocating, the Pereyaslav resident escaped to Wallachian lands.

"And, in accordance with his most zealous wishes, he, Anatoliy, took monastic vows and was shaved by the superior of that Tristen monastery, assuming the rank of robe-bearer."

Anatoliy lived in the monastery until 1745 and, posing as a foreigner, even went to Kiev and then to Poland, to a monastery called Motrenin.

"And, from the aforesaid Motrenin monastery, Anatoliy traveled to the Wallachian city of Bucharest, which had a Hellenic-Greek school."

Here, this man was ordained into monk-priesthood and thence went to live in a monastery at Mount Athos.

"Upon his arrival, he appeared before the superior of the Pavlo-Georgiyevsky monastery, Dosifey, and requested that he, Anatoliy, be admitted to live in that monastery."

He didn't live there long—approximately three months.

Thence, as a man who spoke Greek, Wallachian, and Russian, Anatoliy Meles was sent to Russia to collect voluntary alms in general and, above all, to receive a charitable stipend from the Russian State.

Anatoliy traveled through Constantinople. He brought with him various inexpensive, but marvelous objects: first of all, a piece of a vivifying cross, and second of all—gifts brought to the infant Jesus by the Magi, and so on and so forth.

The Patriarch of Constantinople consecrated Anatoliy as archimandrite.

Thanks to this rank, the runaway seminarian received from the Russian resident Mr. Nepluyev a passport to enter Russia.

In Russia, by order of the Synod, Anatoliy was arrested

following his interrogation.

The Empress herself was informed of this interrogation on February 19, 1760.

Here are some excerpts from the report:

"Being a natural subject of Your Imperial Majesty from the Zolotonosha shtetl of the Pereyaslav regiment of Malorussia, he had, of his own free will, left Russia to travel abroad and, wandering around various places and monasteries in Poland and the Wallachian region, obtained monasticism and priesthood through deceptive means and without having been elected, posing as a cleric of a foreign church; in 1749, he came to Mount Athos, to the Pavlo-Georgiyevsky monastery, and, six months later, was consecrated as archimandrite by the Constantinople Patriarch Kirill in an equally fraudulent manner; he traveled to Russia in 1750 with some sanctity to collect for that monastery a certain charitable sum allocated for the State of Palestine; he received 1,120 rubles from the Synod in the past years and was awarded by none other than Your Imperial Majesty three thousand rubles with an additional one thousand for his travel expenses; moreover, following his, Anatoliy's, request, a Synod decree authorized him to solicit alms for monastery needs and the payment of debts from voluntary donors in the Russian Empire for a period of three years; but he did not provide any notification of the amount he collected in accordance with his binding agreement and did not appear with it at the Synod or the Moscow Synod Office, departing abroad in 1754.

"After his prompt return there in 1755 (evidently by means of his unscrupulous scheme of using those funds toward unholy simony), it pleased a single patriarch to, without any other bishops present for selection, consecrate him as bishop of the denomination of that sole, desolate Meles eparchy, which had neither a bishop's altar, nor any local Christians; he was consecrated by only two bishops."

This was followed by references to the canon.

It turns out that Meles wasn't Meles, and not a bishop, and maybe wasn't even an Anatoliy.

Such purported foreigners were common in Russia at the time.

Famous novelist Fyodor Emin was probably among them . . .

Although Emin didn't pretend to be a bishop.

But astounding events follow in the Synod's report.

Anatoliy was summoned to the ruling Senate.

There, Anatoliy heard a few secret statements concerning higher interests and was released by the Senate.

"Hardly was the aforesaid Anatoliy released abroad by the Senate in 1758 when he, with his usual willfulness, arrived in the Zaporozhian Sech in April 1759 and was admitted by the Zaporozhian Cossacks, who sewed a bishop's vestments for him without any permission from the higher spiritual authority; he willfully ventured, in the guise of a local and legitimate bishop, to perform pontifical services in their church and, moreover, excluded the real eparchial bishop—the Kiev Metropolitan— and replaced his name with his own in the conclusion of his prayer; and thereafter, admitted foreign visitors—vagabond monks like himself—to the church service."

And these monks behaved rowdily at the Sech and didn't minister prayers on Tsarist days. It was as if they were working toward separating the Sech from Russia.

Having received this news, the Senate, too, decided that Anatoliy's sojourn in the Sech was futile and even harmful, and summoned Meles to St. Petersburg to submit him to the will of the spiritual authority.

In the capital, Meles was placed under arrest, interrogated by the Synod and stripped of his bishop's vestments.

It turned out that Anatoliy was conducting talks with the Russian State on removing the Albanians and the Greeks to Russia.

But the State decided against this, fearing war with the

Ottoman Porte.

And Anatoliy said he was detained at the Zaporozhian Sech by chance.

After getting its hands on him, the Synod wasn't merciful.

It decided to send Meles to the Holy Trinity Kondinsky monastery in Siberia.

Monastery jails were the ghastliest.

They drove Meles through Tobolsk.

The Metropolitan of Tobolsk, Pavel, reported to the Synod:

"On the road, Anatoliy, flouting the Most Holy Governing Synod's decisive designation of him, fallaciously proclaimed himself to be bishop, blessed the locals, sought a means for his escape, used various obscene language, and threw a knife at a sentinel for prohibiting him to use such language."

Anatoliy didn't waste away in Siberia. When Catherine ascended to the throne, an order came from her to return the former Bishop to Russia and place him in some monastery with a fitting livelihood.

The Synod carried out the order; Anatoliy was sent to the Zheltovodsky-Makaryev monastery as a simple monk, but was given an allowance triple that of a monk's.

Under the Empress's order, in 1767, Anatoliy was added to the Makaryev monastery's permanent roster of monks.

Soon, however, Anatoliy began to have disagreements with the archimandrite.

Anatoliy fled from the monastery. His features were reported everywhere:

"The aforesaid monk Anatoliy, not slight in height, black eyes, black hair on his head with gray streaks, a scar on the left temple, close to his hair; white face, black and oblong beard; thick-set; speaks Malorussian as well as Greek and Latin."

In the meantime, Anatoliy arrived in Moscow and, the night before December 25, appeared at the Synod Office to petition not to be sent back to the Makaryev monastery. The Synod ordered the Moscow chancery to hold him under arrest and give him 10 kopeks a day for nourishment.

Suddenly, a final order from the Empress arrived summoning Anatoliy. This was on March 16, 1769.

After the tête-à-tête, Catherine bid chief prosecutor Chebyshev to inform the Synod that "she wished for Anatoliy to be forgiven."

Under the pardon, Anatoliy was proclaimed priest again.

The monk-priest Anatoliy fought with Orlov in the Battle of Chesmen.

At that time, it became clear why all his transgressions were pardoned: they needed someone to liaise with the Greeks and the Albanians.

Catherine had ambitious plans for the Mediterranean Sea.

What Anatoliy did on the archipelago is uncertain.

In 1770, the Synod ruled to restore his rank as bishop.

But her ambitious plans didn't succeed.

The navy returned to the Russian ports.

Anatoliy Meles returned as well. He was put away in a closet.

This closet was called the Glukhov monastery.

The story of the canticle

OVER CLINKING CUPS of punch and newly fashionable glasses, the Bishop pronounced that the Synod had been chastened by him, that it couldn't reply to the Prince-Bishop's crafty letters.

A letter from Mr. Ostolopov was received stating that the situation wasn't so dire and was considered rather trivial because the sums collected were commensurate.

But modesty was not a common guest of the Bishop Kirill's.

The guests listened, drank, listened, and recorded because, in the monastery, a letter is a denunciation and a telltale, and it wasn't without reason that Peter, called the Great by many, forbade the monks to write at all.

A rumor traveled to the Synod and a cool wind began to blow from there.

At this time, it was as if Dobrynin's circumstances, too, were shrouded with sadness.

One evening, the gray-haired Rodogozh grandfather walked into the monastic cell.

"My sweet grandson," he said, "there was a fire in our monastery and my house burned down with all my possessions. And that kind woman who lived with me during my widowerhood, not the one you remember, but the other . . ."

At this moment, Gavriil remembered the fever.

"The other one," grandfather said, "quiet, good. Death abducted her, everything died with her. It is not your grandfather who stands before you, it is your grandfather's shadow."

"What do you need, grandpa?"

"Ask the Bishop, Gavriil, tell him: 'my grandfather bows before you and asks for a monk's place in a monastery; he has made peace.'"

A place in the Glinsk hermitage, desolate and poor, was provided to Dobrynin's grandfather by the Bishop.

It was there that grandfather died.

Being a great enemy of idleness, the Bishop spent entire nights over supper with the monastery brethren, chancery members, and the most notorious slanderers invited from town.

They drank, talked, yelled, spoke in syllogisms—that is, various types of righteous conclusions, wrote verses, and played the gusli.

And the former Basilian monk Boniface Boreyko, who was now a Rylsk archimandrite, taught everyone Polish dances.

It was there that they composed replies to the Synod.

But, one day, it occurred to the Bishop to write a poem.

There was already a poem about the chief prosecutor of the Synod Chebyshev, but, unfortunately, it was lost, having been stolen by slanderers for denunciation.

This poem was written in the Polish style and was dedicated to the local Sevsk military chief Pustoshkin.

The poem was seminarian and choppy, with a rich rhyme scheme.

Here it is, with the objectionable parts removed:

Hello, brave fellow,
See, there is an end to honor,
Many reach it with their breast,
Not fearing the deadly road,
To serve the fatherland
And, for that, receive a rank . . .

. . . .

The gentleman finally took into his head
Not to be a flatterer in the service,
Suddenly adopted a patriot's face
To find a reason,
To be known as an honest man,
To become a different man in the civil service . . .

But what meaning could be wished for in poems written over a supper that continued until the old monastery bells struck a commendable hour!

Everyone liked the canticle.

Dobrynin set it to music and, for that, received praise and even a bit of money.

The physician Vints, the same one who treated the drunken archpriest and Dobrynin himself when he had a fever, saw the canticle and most admired the melodiousness of its verses.

With the Bishop's permission, he took the leaflet home to revel in this creation.

The next day, the Bishop came to his senses and sent Gavriil to town to take back the canticle.

The altar boy met Vints as he was leaving his quarters.

"His Grace is asking you to return the canticle."

"I'll send it. At present, I'm going to the Kazan church for mass."

"And I will pray with you," the altar boy said.

"No, why should you wait for me?"

"We pray in church, we don't wait."

In church, the physician assured Dobrynin twice more that he would send the canticle after mass, but it was as if the acolyte was glued to him.

Having returned to his quarters, the physician turned his catalogues over on the table, leafing through a book of folk remedies for cattle, *The Comely Cook*, and his epistle, and said that the canticle fell somewhere and he would return it to the Bishop in person.

The acolyte was forced to return to the monastery.

Gavriil reported that the war chief probably had the canticle.

The Bishop stared pensively and said:

"The canticle was not written by my own hand, but by yours, and it seems to me that you are half its author. And if you have prevented someone from praying in church, then you should have also known how to steal the canticle."

The next day, the doctor returned the canticle after all.

But the war chief read the canticle and reckoned that Dobrynin had composed it.

Still, the Bishop was sometimes visited by the muse. Then, it would seem like he had removed his silk robe and become someone who was meek and pure of heart, but dishonest.

When the war chief visited the Bishop in person to complain about the canticle composed by Dobrynin, Kirill suddenly laughed and said:

"I wrote the canticle myself and very poorly, which is why I won't acknowledge it."

But the war chief didn't retract his denunciation.

The commission established by imperial order arrived, consisting of Chernigov Bishop Theophile, archimandrite Antoniy Pocheka of the Gamaleyev monastery, and two civilians—a colonel and a major.

Furthermore, it turned out that not only the Bishop, but also the war chief, had to be questioned about the denunciation.

And it was necessary to question Nazarka the sexton as a witness, but he was found hanging from a new rope in his confinement.

The Bishop fights back

ACCORDING TO DENUNCIATION rules, first, one must lie down in bed and claim to be ill, collecting information through scribes about the exact nature of the accusation, what reports were filed, and who the witnesses were. Then either remove, send away, or bribe the witnesses, or something else.

But the Bishop didn't stick to his guns. He lay down in bed, but when the commission came to his door with the town doctor for an inspection, instead of declaring to their faces that he was ill (the law stipulated that they had to believe him because he represented the priesthood and one has to believe a bishop), the Bishop jumped out of bed as soon as he saw the doctor and, grabbing him by the collar, yelled:

"I'm a bishop and not a peasant, you must believe me and not testify against me!"

But the commission replied warmly:

"We didn't come to testify against you, but to express our regret and respect with regard to your illness."

The Bishop was ashamed and didn't lie down in bed, but chatted and ran around the chambers.

At that moment, Dobrynin decided to cheer up His Grace.

Prior to the death of Mr. Kasagov, who was so hastily buried without medical verification, his closest servants were set free, and one of them knew how to light fireworks.

Searching for a livelihood, this servant arrived at the Bishop's home.

Dobrynin secretly built fireworks with him.

They were made of different components: tricks, rockets, and Roman candles, and even traced out His Grace's monogram— K. F.—with multicolored lights.

And, when the Bishop was at his most brooding, the altar boy came to him and said:

"Your Grace, would you like to see some festive lights?"

At this moment, the maroons and Roman candles began to explode, the wheels began to spin and Fliorinsky's Parisian soul grew merry; he bade that they serve wine from the cellars, and the wheels of life spun on.

In return for this diversion, Gavriil was appointed clerk.

The visiting commission neither lowered His Grace's rank nor restricted his freedom, and in 1774, in midsummer, His Grace set off to restore propriety in his eparchy. And the cart drove off again to inspect how Mr. Safonov was in fact living.

In any event, they wrote from St. Petersburg that the Bishop was imprudent and it would be preferable if he sang in a lower register and from another canticle, or else he might end up with a monk's serving. And a monk's serving was the name of the poorly cooked gruel and fish that was fed to low-ranking monks.

By now, he needed to repent something without admitting everything.

There was no time to reflect on this. Safonov was hosting a lengthy feast in his hall.

The Putivl superior Manuil Levitsky was almost invariably present at the host's feasts.

An enormous musical orchestra was booming, but the bandmaster conducted out of time and inattentively, believing himself a highly ranked individual because his wife sang well and was the master's lover.

Dissonant music rang out.

The Bishop, who was drinking out of sorrow and out of joy, walked up to the orchestra and shouted:

"Play!"

And the bandmaster, who was drinking out of sorrow and saw his wife sitting on the master's lap, yelled:

"Don't play!"

Some played, others didn't, and confusion ensued.

Everyone started talking and screaming; on the Bishop's side, the choirboys and the superior stood up.

The Bishop started yelling something derogatory about the host.

The host stood up swaying like a smoky pillar and, grabbing the Bishop by the robe, yelled:

"Dogs!"

Oh, hunting with hounds!

A dog needs a vast field where it can leap.

In France, in order to keep a country dog from running, they'd tie a log or a stick to its neck.

The right to hunt with hounds in country fields is a feudal right, and the French Revolution rose against it.

Oh, hunting with hounds!

How many rabbits were hunted, how many wolves and, sometimes, as a special treat, they hunted peasants, and, on a rare occasion, the clergy, because the nobility thought that the priests' robes were especially alluring bait for dog fangs.

Oh, the liberties of noblemen!

Bishops were not hunted by dogs, which is why the spectacle we presently behold was both factual and extraordinary.

Think about it: had it been long since the patriarch reigned with the sovereign?

Had it been long since Peter I escaped to hide in the Trinity Lavra of St. Sergius, had it been long since the monasteries established robust feudal economies on their vast fields?

It was only recently that fairs bustled on monastery lands, only recently that the clergy held a third of all the land.

Sic transit gloria mundi.

The land passed through the Empress's hands to the gentry.

At this time, shouts interrupt our digression.

"Dogs!" yelled the drunken Safonov to the sounds of the drunken dissonant orchestra playing a minuet.

The Bishop did not wait to be pursued by hounds and hopped over the table, preaching as he ran:

"In case you are chased out of one city, run to another, shaking off your feet the ash that clings to you."

Dobrynin ran directly behind him and snatched a silver candlestick from the table in case he'd have to fight off the dogs.

Dobrynin ran vigorously, chanting:

"Guide my footsteps according to your word."

Behind him, the clergy and choirboys ran in a loose formation, shouting in various vocal timbres.

Safonov remained alone on the battlefield. The dogs were far away.

He took the bandmaster's wife by the hand.

The orchestra began to play the ceremonial march and set off, accompanying the master to the bedchamber's doors.

At that moment, the doors closed, and what the orchestra played before the closed doors, I do not know.

The Bishop ran down the village street to the archpriest's house.

At night, he slept soundly and didn't cry out.

In the morning, a courier was sent to Safonov's house to recover the Bishop's staff, which they failed to grab the previous day.

When he returned, the messenger reported that the master had unwittingly met him in the hall entrance.

Safonov was wearing a shirt, shoes, and nothing else.

Scratching himself, Safonov inquired about the Bishop's health and, finding out that His Grace was leaving, howled:

"Oh, I thought he was going to dine with me! My coach! My breeches! Bath! Chase!"

Wishing to be chased, the Bishop set off as soon as possible.

On the road, Fliorinsky saw dust rise on the horizon and ordered that his horses be whipped mercilessly.

The Bishop's carriage flew through the villages with a ruckus.

The villages flashed by.

Crows flew off the trees like splashes of water off the road.

But Safonov's horses were overtaking them.

The Bishop arrived in the village—Safonov was there.

The Bishop entered a peasant's izba—Safonov was in the courtyard.

He asked to be let in, assuring the Bishop that neither the bandmaster nor the bandmaster's wife nor the dogs were with him and that he would chase him like a shadow chases the body.

After he was let in, Safonov got on his knees and covered his face with a kerchief to show that his plea for forgiveness was tearful.

As he wept, a basket with wine was brought in, to which the Bishop reacted by saying:

"Gavriil, open the cellarette!"

They began to irrigate a peace treaty.

They drank, drank, and scolded.

Safonov yelled:

"Dogs!"

But no one was frightened.

There were no dogs.

They left.

In a month or two, they found out that Safonov had drunk to excess and died.

Not a revengeful man, the Bishop came to bury the deceased.

He sang over him with the entire choir, gave a speech, and, for that, His Grace received a large fee from his relatives because he had absolved the deceased of all his sins.

Again, they came to the Petropavlovsky-Glukhov monastery to visit the merry Greek Anatoliy Meles.

The summer night was balmy.

The frogs were croaking. In the distant, non-monastic forest, the bittern was shrieking.

They drank, drank, and fired from cannons, then decided to ring the remaining bells.

Gavriil, who loved the sound of ringing bells, climbed atop the bell tower and rang them with the choirboys, beating the bells with sticks.

And the bells were famous, they were cast by St. Dmitry of Rostov, who was a great aficionado of the sound of ringing bells as well as horses.

The bittern was shrieking, the frogs were shrieking to compete with the bells, Anatoliy Meles was singing in Greek, Kirill Fliorinsky was singing in French, and Dobrynin was ringing the bells.

At that moment, the Holy Synod commission arrived.

A report had been filed that Anatoliy loves to fire cannons, never gets dressed, always walks around barefoot, and imprisons monks without justification.

Paisiy, the archimandrite of the Lubensky monastery, and Joseph, the superior of the Gustynsky monastery, arrived and brought a provisional superior with them.

In the blink of an eye, Anatoliy sobered up, ceased firing the cannons, put on his boots, washed his face, chewed on aloe resin, which brings a drunk man back to his senses and wards off odors, put on his robe, covered his head with a monastic cowl, hung a panagia on his neck, and wound amber beads around his hand.

Anatoliy was a wise and eloquent person.

When he arrived at the Bishop's, he threw himself at his feet and uttered:

"Preceptor! Save me, I'm ruined!"

The archimandrite replied:

"Fool, why do you disbelieve? I am being prosecuted for bribes, church looting, and wenches, but I don't lose my nerve."

They wrote their replies together and, taking Anatoliy along, the Bishop traveled to Glukhov and submitted the clauses to the collegiate councilor Kozelsky.

Seeing how magnificent Anatoliy Meles looked wearing boots and with his hair combed, Kozelsky said:

"Your Grace, oh, how this magnificent appearance suits you! Why don't you always dress this way! Then, you would call on us, we would call on you, and we would pass the time in the most heavenly way. After all, your discourse before her Imperial Majesty is renowned, it was you who brought glory to the Empress and your deeds would not be deemed offensive were they not noisy. Really, why did you have to fire the cannons?"

To which Anatoliy replied:

"And why didn't you warn me? The Greeks have a saying: 'Where wine is spilt, so are words' and, perhaps, more than one deed of mine has bathed in wine. I beheld Russian ships between the islands scattered on the Mediterranean Sea. These ships resembled a new archipelago. Their cannons are like thunder. So I fell in love with cannons, to which my fate is bound."

To mark this occasion, they decided to drink.

But there were fireworks in the Bishop's cart.

They drank—and, suddenly, there was a crackling, a hubbub, and the wheels began to turn.

The ladies shrieked and the Sevsk Bishop lit a Roman candle, threw it at the Petropavlovsky Bishop, and singed his beard.

The beard crackled, the bonnets and toques, that is to say, ladies, lamented, and their cries rose to heaven.

When the smoke settled, they found Prosecutor Semyonov in a pitiful state. Having a predisposition to stroke, he almost died. He was brought to his senses with poultices.

Regaining consciousness, the prosecutor declared that such pranks were against the law because they could be lethal.

To which Fliorinsky retorted:

"My son, there was no better occasion for you to serve as the custodian of the law than in this smoke because you'd have been buried by two Bishops who are both indicted by the court."

On events taking place outside the monastery

EVERY SPRING, AN apple tree bloomed in the monastery courtyard.

Every spring, an elder tree bloomed by the monastery wall. Then, all this was overgrown by nettles.

All the roads in the monastery were familiar. By now, the rebuilt church was beginning to decay.

The Bishop's miters, which were fashioned from St. Nicholas the Wonder-worker's robes, were already growing old.

There, outside the walls, life continued and changed.

They were dividing up Poland; they didn't divide it straightaway, but several times.

They negotiated with the Chartoriysky family, bargained with Friedrich of Prussia, and conceded land to Austria.

And Maria Theresa, the Austrian Empress, felt pangs of conscience at night and demanded new allotments.

Count Chernyshev wished for the borders to lie along the Dnieper and Dvina rivers, absorbing Polish Livonia, Dinaburg, Polotsk, and the Polotsk province.

The Polish primate demanded up to one hundred thousand rubles for his assistance.

In the meantime, they needed to hurry and pay off a certain someone in Belarus, and significant funds had also been allocated during the days of the Empress Elizabeth for the repair of St. Stanislav's Cathedral in Mogilev—ten thousand and six hundred rubles in silver coins.

And a stipend of five hundred rubles for the Mogilev bishop.

This Bishop, the famous Georgiy Konissky, who was a friend of Fliorinsky, gave a notable speech upon receiving the stipend.

At the time, he was still a Polish citizen.

I won't quote the speech in full because our views on eloquence have changed and this speech may not be a paragon of it.

But its excerpts are remarkable:

"Having received the highest favor from Your Imperial Majesty in the form of the allocated monetary sum for the completion of the church and the upkeep of the seminary in addition to my annual stipend, I hazard, with this dastardly epistolet, to convey my obsequious gratitude to Your Imperial Majesty."

And further on:

"I have so many more reasons to worship the same Christ the Lord now that Your Imperial Majesty, who has grown to love the Savior, has most graciously granted the aforesaid sum toward the completion of his temple rather than merely pay him lip service."

And the aforesaid letter was signed:

"Your most loyal slave and pedestal Georgiy of Belarus."

The project progressed to its conclusion.

Russia was advancing to the southern ports.

Mogilev was situated on the Dnieper, which flowed into the Black Sea.

At that time, rivers were more attractive than they are now.

Russia was advancing to the sea and, on the way, defeated

the Zaporozhian Sech. The Sech raged, but it was weak.

Year after year, the steppes were settled.

Year after year, the monastery grew quieter, the apple tree blossomed, and the Bishop Kirill, who wasn't in his rightful place, was useless to the Empress, and didn't give brilliant speeches, grew older.

The Bishop's power weakened even over Dobrynin.

Gavriil moved his belongings to a separate chamber. He began to complete his education and read the multi-volume *Roman History* in Mr. Tredyakovsky's translation. He read *The Adventures of Telemachus* and the poems of Mr. Sumarokov, as well as those of many others.

But above all, he loved Mr. Chulkov's *The Comely Cook*, Kurganov's *Letter Writer*, and even the works of Voltaire and Montesquieu, which instilled in him a definitive contempt for monastic writings.

Trouble was brewing in the Bishop's home.

The Bishop quarreled with the Trubchev voivode Kolyubakin and splashed a glass of wine in his eyes; in return Kolyubakin struck him so forcefully in his ear that the hierarch had to be carried out on the arms of the parish clergy.

The next day, Kolyubakin came and half-drunkenly kneeled in the middle of the monastery, by the apple tree.

It was August and apples hung off the apple tree.

Kolyubakin, who had digestive problems, gazed at them greedily and then screamed loudly:

"Father, I have sinned against heaven and before thee!"

Looking out the window, the Bishop answered:

"Say it, you mangy sheep: 'Lord have mercy on me'—and stand there."

In the Bishop's chambers, an exceptional denunciation was being written with references to the *Book of the Helmsman* and the ordinances and a remark that the Bishop was not bareheaded, but wore a skullcap on his head and a panagia on his chest, and was dressed in his angelic armor, so to speak.

Kolyubakin, drunk and weary from thirst, knelt before the tree and chewed on a fallen apple.

He was finally called to the chambers, where he tearfully explained that they had both been inebriated.

They buried the hatchet on the condition that Kolyubakin would also repent at the Sevsk Bishop's home.

But Kolyubakin didn't come a second time.

Then, the Bishop repudiated Kolyubakin's household, which is to say he excommunicated it from the Church.

The archpriest took the Bishop's missive to the voivode.

The latter served him tea, which marked the end of the tragedy.

Fliorinsky was going through a difficult time. Life was in full swing, the State expanded and the nobility's assets multiplied. The Sevsk monastery was clearly insulated from all this.

The Synod wrote to the Bishop that he should personally request his covenant, meaning his retirement.

But, in response, the Bishop wrote fervently about his education and the fact that no one could be his teacher.

The Synod replied caustically:

"You write with much fervor, and your fervor can cool any heart."

At that moment, the despairing Bishop decided to marry off Dobrynin.

Kirill had a niece, a beautiful girl of fourteen. His Grace called Gavriil and said to him:

"Oh child, my spirit is weary, incline your ear to me."

This was done.

"Marry Sofya and I will care for you as if you were my own son."

And suddenly, he cried out in anger:

"Marry immediately!"

Dobrynin replied evasively and received a signet engagement

ring from the Bishop, but the ring had a precious diamond in it, also from St. Nicholas the Wonder-worker.

But time passed, Gavriil courted the girl and some sort of feeling even touched his soul. There were few women in the monastery and Sofya was young. But a terrible rumor ran; it was as if the Bishop was no longer a Bishop.

Why tie yourself to a wounded horse?

And Gavriil bided his time, didn't give his word and postponed the wedding date to Lent.

It was nighttime and everyone was sleeping; Gavriil was asleep when he heard a knock on the door. And the Bishop's voice.

Familiar with the Bishop's ways and the monastery rods, Gavriil decided not to capitulate.

He grabbed the rifle that Kasagov had given to him as a gift, stuck the barrel out the window, and yelled:

"Whoever takes me on will be met by a bullet!"

A clerk, Matvey Samoylov, stepped out of the crowd and said:

"I advise you to capitulate."

But Gavriil responded:

"I'm not so miserable yet as to require your advice."

"Come out of there," Samoylov continued, "the Bishop has already gone to sleep."

The Bishop was indeed asleep, and when he awoke the next morning, he left, ordering them to pile snow before Gavriil's room.

It was early winter, but there was already snow on the ground.

The blizzard stretched thinly across the ground, resembling the fabric they place on the faces of the dead.

The Bishop was somber.

He stopped his carriage.

The temperature was lower than negative twenty degrees Celsius.

"Serve me some beer. Now sing: 'It is Truly Meet and Right to Bless Thee, O Theokotos . . .'"

The blizzard swept across the ground and the wind blew from the horizon as if from underneath a door.

The beer froze in the Bishop's glass.

The choirboys' hair was covered with white frost, the horses' hair was silver with rime, the treble voices sang and wept, and the cunning basses hummed so as not to open their mouths.

"Sing, you bastards!" the Bishop shouted. "I cannot forsake your voices!"

Chapter on monastery events

AT THE MONASTERY, Gavriil woke up and tried the door, but it was blocked by snow.

He wanted to eat, the day was fading.

A winter day is short and one wants to eat.

He needed to devise a course of action.

Gavriil took the diamond ring off his finger, wrapped it in paper, and wrote in his handwriting on the other, clerical paper:

"Your Holy Grace! The ring you had given me as a token of the nuptials that were to take place between your niece and me, I return as a sign of my eternal separation from her, you, and the entire world."

Then, Dobrynin took Bakhtin's pistol, sat at the window, and began to load it.

Gavriil threw this missive out of the casement, shouting to the watchman and showing a pistol through the window.

The monastery community loves events; they went searching for the Bishop and found him with the choirboys not far from the monastery.

The choirboys were no longer singing but croaking, and the Bishop, too, looked weary.

After reading the note, the Bishop cried out:

"Drive!"

Hardly an hour passed before the Bishop knocked on Gavriil's door.

"Are you alive, Absalom? Quit fooling around, open up!"

The talks began and Gavriil asked for a written dismissal and a discharge certificate from the chancery. These papers were served to him through the window on pitchforks.

Then, the Bishop was admitted; he was gentle and weary, and asked why Gavriil was opposed to the marriage.

"If I enter into matrimony with your niece," said Gavriil, "I fear I will commit incest, so to speak."

Fliorinsky remained silent.

The departure of the Russian Gil Blas Dobrynin

DOBRYNIN'S BRIDE PASSED away during Lent in 1777.

Having grieved for a bit, Dobrynin began to make final preparations for his departure.

He had a friend, the nobleman Lutsevin, who had served in the Rylsk voivode's chancery.

He was beaten with sticks before the Secretary for copying a petition from the citizens to the Senate.

Lutsevin was beaten with sticks and the Secretary looked on, laughing indifferently and sniffing tobacco.

Afterward, Lutsevin sat in heavy fetters.

And he was placed in fetters out of pity because, given the lack of furnishings in prisons at the time, they placed the prisoners' legs in logs and locked those logs. For this reason, they were called convicts in stocks.

And they would gather several people in a single log, both men and women. Dobrynin pitied the prisoner.

Lutsevin got out of fetters and transferred to the Sevsk

chancery with the rank of clerk.

There, he befriended Gavriil, and together they read *The Comely Cook* and *Gil Blas*, and dreamt of faraway travels.

Dobrynin had one thousand three hundred rubles, silver coins, a fox fur coat, and a silver snuffbox with a false bottom.

Restless days began for the Bishop—the Synod's replies were marked by a contemptuous tone.

He said good-bye to his assistant, adding with a smile:

"If you're better off, you won't remember me, if you're worse off—you will."

Then, he was engrossed by some short French novel again.

The horses galloped and turned away from the monastery, and the gates disappeared.

The towers flanked them on one side as the carriage crossed an echoing bridge.

Dobrynin stood up in the carriage and looked at the town, at the Bishop's house.

A bell sang and bobbed under the wheeler's bow.

Dobrynin said with anguish:

"Good-bye, the town of Sevsk and the Bishop's house; good-bye, pleasant minutes that flew by as if they never were; good-bye, the Bishop's bitter wine and unsteady love! Here, behind the wall, I received the knowledge of the cubic root and Roman history and the story of the human heart."

And Lutsevin, who was a bit drunk, as befit a nobleman, began to sing an unintelligible song about roads that must perish and overgrow.

The coachman turned around and saw that the gentlemen were not too generous, but would tip him the first time around.

He struck the horses, the off-wheelers galloped and shook their bells, and the versts began to flash by like beads on a monastery rosary as they turned toward a far-off grove, setting the pace.

They spent the night at an inn marked by a chopped-down

fir tree rather than a shingle.

"Where are we going?" Dobrynin asked.

"To a place where they'll pay us and won't strike us too hard with sticks," Lutsevin answered.

"I don't like military service," Dobrynin said, "there is a war on now and they will make us seize trenches or fight with Janissaries."

"Yes," Lutsevin said, "military officers fancy themselves princes, but they're as bare as tambourines . . . Even my grandfather," Lutsevin continued, "signed up to be a guild master when Tsar Peter called the nobles for a military inspection."

"So you are not a nobleman at present?"

"Not in the least."

Dobrynin was a bit disappointed and said pensively:

"And I may come from Pereyaslav gentry." After a silence, he added: "But we must obtain ranks, and not out of vanity: there are many fertile lands propitious to growing hemp, but only nobles can own serfs. Isn't it insulting to see people at Ukrainian fairs, and among them attractive women, who are sold separately, one at a time and at a low price . . . to see them and not have the right to buy them?"

"Our condition is insulting to humanity."

"A third social class is not thriving in our country, if you want to live—be a nobleman."

"Only nobility makes our air easier to breathe and somewhat Parisian," Lutsevin added, "and entitles one to a sword. We need ranks."

They both fell silent.

"Wouldn't it be nice to be a clerk or a scribe for a wealthy builder or tax farmer?"

The off-wheelers' bells, the tin bells, rang: "Wouldn't it be nice, wouldn't it be nice?"

"That would be wonderful!" Lutsevin said. "They are acquainted with highly placed gentlemen and the General-

Prosecutor, through whom they not only request titles for themselves, but have the chance to do so for others. Particularly when they enter into contracts at the Senate."

In the distance, villages covered with straw roofs flashed by and black smoke drifted from the small windows under those roofs like vapor from mouths.

The villages were far away.

From afar, church crosses flickered like sparks and the road raced under them.

"Wouldn't it be nice, wouldn't it be nice?" resounded the off-wheelers' tin bells. And the bell under the wheeler's bow replied to them in a bass tone.

"I wish," Dobrynin said, out of time with the ringing, "to work in a customs house: there would be money, felt, linen, materials, and loads of other fancy and exquisite goods. And you could also request titles and buy peasants."

At that moment, all the bells began to ring at once, the carriage rode downhill, and Lutsevin said effusively:

"Belarus has been annexed to our empire, divided into two halves and fully absorbed by Russian provinces. At present, two governorates have been established. The Pskov governorate, which consists of five provinces: Pskov, Velikolutsk, Dvinsk, Polotsk, and Vitebsk. There is also a Mogilev governorate, which is split into three provinces: Mogilev, Orsha, and Rogachev. And Count Chernyshev has been appointed Governor-General of both. An order was issued to endow residents of the newly annexed lands with rights equivalent to those of long-standing Russian subjects so as to eradicate any grounds for claims to some sort of eternal privileges."

The coachman shouted, the horses galloped.

Lutsevin said:

"According to an edict from her Imperial Majesty, the governors will personally appoint officers without consulting the Senate. They need people. At present, Pyotr Zvyagin is the director of the Rogachev customs house, and he was once a clerk like me."

The coachman was shouting, the bridges were rattling.

Far away, the glittering crosses were already turning red because the sun was setting.

The bells were ringing: rank, rank, rank, rank . . .

Newly acquired land

The roads in Belarus are smooth and planted with birch trees on both sides.

This was ordered by Count Zakhar Grigoryevich Chernyshev.

The postal office in Belarus is in good working order, the houses are newly built, and horses are harnessed deftly and fearfully.

Postal workers wear green felt jackets, copper crests on their foreheads, and a number on their temple.

Everything is new. The new broom sweeps well.

And the bridges don't dance across the entire breadth of the road, don't rattle, only hum.

But the town of Rogachev is unseemly.

The buildings are gray.

The Roman Catholic Church, the Eastern Catholic Church, and the synagogue with the tall, steep roof.

The deserted castle ramparts, overgrown by grass, the sandy mounds in the middle of town, and the old wooden Catholic church on the bank of the Dnieper.

Here, the Drut River flows into the Dnieper and, on a narrow cape called a horn in Belarusian, on a narrow bank, stands the town of Rogachev.

When Dobrynin rode into this town, it was funded solely by the State.

First, our fortune-seekers sought out Zvyagin.

It took some time for Zvyagin to recognize Lutsevin.

They sifted through many memories, recalled voivodes' chanceries and acquaintances, and finally remembered each other.

But our travelers received a hearty welcome.

At lunch, Zvyagin said:

"You have acted prudently: you won't amount to anything sitting at home, and here, there is room, so to speak, and they're not too discriminate. I have a benefactor, Sergey Kozmich Vyazmitinov, he knew me when I was still a steward."

Here, Dobrynin was overjoyed:

"Does he come from Rylsk landowners? I knew a second lieutenant named Ivan Vyazmitinov."

"That is his younger brother," Zvyagin answered. "But let us start at the beginning. As everyone knows, our customs duties may bolster the fortune of a careful man, but our post is slippery and destructive for one who longs to grow rich. I am thankful to God that, having respected the obligations of my office and the importance of the oath of allegiance, I am neither indicted nor investigated and have hope for the future."

The fortune-seekers were pleased with this conversation.

Lutsevin said:

"We are careful and experienced people. Tell us, is your staff full?"

"It is full," Zvyagin answered. "But will it be full tomorrow? You need to speak to someone, a Mr. Khamkin. He is on good terms with the chancery superior Aleyevtsev, who may serve any document to the Governor."

They spent the next day dashing around. The cohorts met remarkable people.

For instance, they recognized the customs clerk Kiselevsky, the former valet of the Sevsk voivode.

At present, he already had his freedom and his sword.

They also recognized a certain man in a dress coat of light-gray camlet.

This man turned out to be Prince Gorchakov, who served with the former valet and advised them to work for the prosecutor and not the customs house.

Old man Khamkin gave our friends a cool welcome and showed them parcels addressed in his name.

The parcels were indeed addressed to "His Honor Mr. Khamkin."

Prince Gorchakov received Dobrynin and Lutsevin without ceremony. A four-course lunch was served.

At lunch, the host sat with his lover Parasha, a wayward woman who wasn't coarse-natured.

After lunch, the Prince's servant Nikashka played the gusli and Parasha sang, and, at that moment, Dobrynin showed the extent of his abilities and the Bishop's training, and sang both by ear and from sheet music.

After lunch, Lutsevin went to sleep.

But, being a man of experience, Dobrynin was not knocked out by the wine and went for a stroll in the pinewood, wandering on the banks of the Drut and the Dnieper.

The river breeze blew away his inebriation.

At six o'clock, Dobrynin was at Vyazmitinov's house with a mind as clear as glass.

Vyazmitinov, a man of advanced years in dignified dress, received Dobrynin and said benevolently:

"We need people, we're settling the land with Russians, so to speak. But I cannot offer any posts except one with a hundred-ruble salary. If you need rank more than you need a salary, I promise to request this post for you."

"Don't throw away your first stroke of luck," Dobrynin thought, and replied with a bow as low as the human frame allowed.

"Your Honor is aware that, in Russia, a man without a rank

is almost like a man without a soul. If you give me preference, I will not seek another post."

"Alright, write a request in due form."

"Your Honor, allow me to travel to Mogilev after I submit this request."

"What is there for you to do?"

"Knowledge of the governorate's principal town is indispensable to service and I also need to see my friend off."

"Why are you fussing about him? I heard that, when he was young, he was already involved in writing denunciations."

"I haven't heard this; however, it may be true and it may be slander. He isn't old yet, and time will teach him how to dwell with people on Earth."

Thus spoke Dobrynin, remembering the monastery rule: "Do not hasten to betray."

"Everything is possible," Vyazmitinov said. "But go to Mogilev and bring me a bucket or two of cherries, we didn't get any this year."

At ten in the morning, the request was submitted and the voivode accepted it; after reading it, he said:

"Very good. We need good people."

In the request, Dobrynin specified almost by chance that he was issued from Malorussian gentry.

And again, the Belarusian roads ran below him, dappled with shadows from newly planted birch trees.

Belarusian fields stood out through the white birch trunks.

In Mogilev, lunches were pathways.

The town overflowed with various sorts of young men with posts.

At lunch, they decided two things.

First: to drink a bit of Polish honey.

This honey instantly deprived the friends of their feet, but not of their lucidity.

It was also decided that Lutsevin would enter service and,

at the opening of the governorate administration, wouldn't seek a low position and wouldn't miss a chance to acquire titles because, in these parts, they were valuable people.

The next day, fortune smiled on Lutsevin.

He called Vice-Governor Voronin His Excellency and the latter recalled Lutsevin's relatives and engaged him directly.

Lutsevin's noblesse was never mentioned in conversation.

The cathedral built on Empress Elizabeth's funds was immense, white, and empty.

Although it was a holiday, the governorate chancery was crowded, teeming with a multitude of middling civil servants and newly appointed chief officers.

New silver braids and buttons shone.

People laughed, strolled about as if they were at a market, sprinkled their powdered hair with sand from sandboxes, and frolicked in various ways.

Lutsevin joined this horde immediately and, afterward, advanced with success, which, perhaps, will be alluded to later.

Dobrynin, who hadn't yet received a rank, left the merry Mogilev feeling a bit sad.

He didn't forget to buy two buckets of cherries and poured them into a barrel.

There was Rogachev again and the steep roof of the synagogue and Jews in long coats and white stockings. There was the river again, flowing dully into the Dnieper.

At first, Vyazmitinov received Dobrynin with interest.

"Now, show me the cherries," he said.

The barrel was presented.

"My friend," Vyazmitinov said, "a miserly but intelligent man would have covered the cherries with cherry leaves and they wouldn't have gotten crushed on the road. A wise man would have poured French vodka over the cherries, which is sold in Mogilev for four rubles a bucket. A careless and negligent man brought crushed cherries. I am sad to say that you will have to wait a while for your rank."

Service, stanzas, and sleds . . .

VYAZMITINOV, WHO DIDN'T give Dobrynin a rank, traveled to Rylsk to visit his father.

Gavriil remained alone in the chancery; the chancery was located in an izba whose owner had already been retitled a chancery attendant.

In the dark cell where the chancery table stood, black cockroaches scurried around that had not been retitled yet.

Having filled and sealed all the crevices, particularly around the doorway and window jambs, and then whitewashed them, Dobrynin got to work in this sanctuary of justice without much joy.

There was a chest in the chancery and, in the chest, lay dossiers that hadn't been inscribed in the register.

There was virtually nothing to do. And, at Gorchakov's, Parasha sang well, the gusli player played, and, for the first time in his life, Dobrynin sang for his own pleasure, though admittedly, in exchange for free wine.

Mr. Shpynev, a student of the celebrated Lomonosov, came here frequently. He was an uncommonly educated man.

And Dobrynin himself could distinguish iambic verse from a trochee and knew what a long rhyme and a rich rhyme were.

Only an incomplete knowledge of mythology kept him from writing poetry.

But here, the excellent dictionary of mythology came to our friends' rescue.

As for Shpynev, he wrote his poems without mythology.

He composed poems about the various kinds of people in the town.

For example, he wrote a poem about Mr. Khamkin:

The master here is more long-winded than a throat
That wails in God's temple without receiving any alms.

Mr. Khamkin was infuriated by this poem and considered it worthless.

The voivode Maleyev also looked askance at our friends.

Dobrynin was asked to come to the public chancery with everyone else and, perhaps, this would have been the end of Mr. Dobrynin—because they now called him Mister—had he not been reading a book called *The art of prudent behaviour, in a father's advice to his son.*

It was an interesting book. Shpynev had given it to Dobrynin.

And when Gorchakov saw Parasha looking at Dobrynin, he bitterly marked Aristippus's speech in the book with his nail:

"You are aware that a noble title endows one with sophisticated thoughts and bars one from any lowly affairs. And all immediate tasks of chamber service are contemptible in the eyes of nobles. You must bow before anyone of higher rank and crawl before eminent landowners, and, moreover, obtain access to eminent persons, whose chamber servants creep in through lackeys, women, and boyars, all of which is low, detestable, and repulsive to nobility."

And further:

"Anyone who enters chamber service out of poverty and low birth shall, without shame and scruples, enter any, and particularly advantageous, schemes with the knowledge that he couldn't be any poorer or worse off than he already is."

After hearing these words, Dobrynin took his tobacco box out of his pocket, played with it distractedly, and said in a dull voice:

"Yes, enlightenment . . ."

When he came home, Dobrynin sat down to write verses and wrote until morning, and, in the morning, saw that his verses were about Shpynev and not Gorchakov.

He had left these verses as if by accident on the table of the public chancery.

The prosecutor read them without distraction.

In the evening, Dobrynin had already been invited into the company of the highest-ranked civil servants in town and given an entrance glass, and here he read the verses and everyone laughed a lot.

These were the verses:

Whose muddled head, eyes, and face grow sour,
Whose paunch sags over his legs and over his nose—his brow?
Hiding his putrid corpse in a malodorous hut,
Trembling crapulously and yawning fiercely with his mouth,
It is the famous Shpynev, who writes verses about one and all
Without perceiving his drunken sins and own flaw.

Since then, Dobrynin's fortune improved and he wasn't even required to sit in the chancery anymore, but took advantage of this leniency with moderation.

Dobrynin continued to visit the Prince, but was now treated with sobriety and aloofness.

His benefactor Vyazmitinov returned from his holiday by taking the first winter road.

Upon his return, he called Dobrynin over and asked:

"Do you have a lot of money left in Sevsk?"

"About one thousand rubles. But it is difficult to collect it all at once because I have invested it."

"You should bring it here, you will earn three hundred percent interest. I will arrange it."

Dobrynin understood this meant that it would earn quadruple interest and said:

"It would be better if I went to Sevsk with a new rank."

At the age of twenty-six, Dobrynin was declared in an order to be a collegiate registrar and could finally insert his sword in his caftan pocket.

It was as if even Rogachev began to look completely different.

And his rank was merely that of a provincial protocol scribe.

Dobrynin received an order to visit Rylsk upon his return from Sevsk to call on Vyazmitinov's relatives and firmly promised himself to fulfill all instructions.

Here is Sevsk again and the Seva River under blue ice. And here are both parts of the town—the town and the Zamaritskaya section—and there, the Maritsa River. In the winter, it resembles a ravine.

There is the flour mill steaming over the dam.

"Hello, Sevsk! I didn't even see you before."

Ten taverns. A row of hotels, forty-three shops, three town churches. And here is the Trinity convent with its four towers, and inside, two stone churches and seventeen nuns.

Good thing Dobrynin didn't remain in the monastery.

And here are the paint-grinding factories and, finally, the Spassky monastery and stone wall and two churches—one made of stone and one of wood—the very same from which Dobrynin carried out wood chips.

The Bishop wasn't at the monastery. The Bishop was in Orlov.

Dobrynin visited his mother and performed various motions with his sword before her, and she exclaimed happily.

Others were less excited about the sword, and secretaries muttered that ranks received at the governorate were not real ranks, but acting ranks.

But wisdom already nested in Dobrynin's heart.

It wasn't for nothing that he had already read *The art of prudent behaviour* as well as Baltasar Gracián's *The Courtier's Manual Oracle Or The Art of Prudence* and many other useful books.

In Rylsk, he bought a fashionable sled for five imperials. At the time, five imperials was not a trifling sum.

The sled was lacquered with light-green paint and inlaid with bronze in the proper places; the pillows were velveteen and the rug was bearskin.

Dobrynin placed this sleigh on top of another, laborer's sleigh, so that it wouldn't break on the way. And he placed boxes of English beer on the sleigh and covered the boxes with hay, recalling the fate of the Mogilev cherries.

As for the money, he hid it because he was quite capable of collecting quadruple interest himself.

The road was good and smooth. The sky was blue and the fur coat was warm. They reached Rogachev safely.

Ivan Kozmich Vyazmitinov received Mr. Dobrynin with interest.

And asked immediately:

"Did you bring the money?"

The protocol scribe bowed in the civilian manner and answered:

"Given the briefness and suddenness of my visit, I was only given three hundred, which I am enclosing."

Vyazmitinov grimaced gloomily.

Dobrynin bowed graciously and added:

"To compensate for my deficiency, I brought you a sleigh as a gift."

"You can ride it yourself," Vyazmitinov said sullenly.

They went out in the hall.

An unsolicited smile drew apart the benefactor's venerable lips.

The sleigh had two seats with a third on the rear platform, and was cozy and light.

"I'll need to," Vyazmitinov said, "go see the landowners a-bout a trotter for this sleigh."

And he unfolded the bear rug, repeating:

"What riches! And what is this hay?"

"It's to protect the bottles of English beer."

"Well, brother, you're a great expert at going on holiday, you will grow out of your rank quickly and reach the highest star someday."

To the stars

IN THE SPRING, Lutsevin arrived from Mogilev. And Lutsevin was already a secretary.

While Dobrynin was only a protocol scribe. Even the sky over him turned slightly yellow.

In the meantime, the opening of the Mogilev governorate administration was approaching.

Dobrynin didn't sleep at night and kept putting out and blowing up the fire. And he almost started having nocturnal fits.

"What a sleigh," he said, "and I wasn't the one to ride in it."

But gratitude lived on in Mr. Vyazmitinov's fleshy heart.

Not only did he approve Dobrynin's request for a holiday in Mogilev, but also gave him two letters: one for Colonel Kakhovsky and the other for his brother, the General-Adjutant Vyazmitinov.

Moreover, he kissed Dobrynin on the forehead and said:

"Go off, you fine fellow."

Dobrynin wished to throw himself at his benefactor's feet according to monastery custom, but somehow ran into the hilt of his sword and remained standing.

This was the effect of a noble rank on a man.

Kakhovsky gently took the letter and immediately directed the supplicant to Mr. Aleyevtsev.

Aleyevtsev was a remarkable man.

His speech was laconic, clear, and halting; he knew civil law and already imagined himself a bureaucrat from another era, although he loved to drink and was often taken into custody to sober up.

But wine had not yet made Mr. Aleyevtsev fat; he had lively blue eyes and fair hair, and wasn't overly corpulent, but a bit stout.

After reading Kakhovsky's note, Aleyevtsev asked:

"What is it that you need?"

Dobrynin didn't bow too low so that they wouldn't think he was a gratuitous supplicant and said:

"A rank and a post when the governorate administration opens."

"Very well. You'll get it. Come to the chancery more often."

Dobrynin ran home happily and told Lutsevin about his success.

But the provincial secretary reacted to this news coolly and said:

"You'll keep going and going there . . ."

The chancery was filled with light, order had already set in and people weren't dashing around and pouring sand boxes on each other's heads.

Quills were creaking, paper was rustling, and petitioners spoke in hushed voices.

Dobrynin went there and transcribed what they gave him. A week went by.

Handing the document to Aleyevtsev, Gavriil placed fifty rubles in it.

Aleyevtsev raised his blue eyes at Dobrynin and asked:

"Oh, it's you . . . And what is your name?"

"Gavriil Ivanovich Dobrynin," the protocol scribe replied.

"Alright, Gavriil, I will place you on the roster for the post of the governor's registrar."

A copyist from an adjacent desk listened to this discourse with his neck outstretched.

Aleyevtsev had just left the room when a great uproar rose with yelling and muffled howling.

"For what reason," they said, "was the devil from the swamp placed with the Governor? He only just got here, and we've toiled night and day."

At that moment, Mr. Aleyevtsev returned to the room.

Silence set in. Aleyevtsev sat down in his armchair and, without turning to the civil servants, answered them with his rear, so to speak:

"Shut up, idiots! You can't all be assigned to a single post with the Governor and he needs someone like him."

Then, turning around, he yelled:

"Shut up! Don't talk! Do you have any idea what orthography is?"

Only the squeaking of quills resounded in the chancery for a half-hour.

But Dobrynin didn't have much faith in orthography.

And, in a few days, he submitted his copy with fifty rubles again.

Aleyevtsev looked at him with affection and asked:

"And what is your patronymic?"

"Ivanovich," Dobrynin said.

"Well, Gavriil Ivanovich, I will write a recommendation expressing my approbation for your work and abilities, which have been noted by His Excellency himself, and I will designate you . . . On the other hand, let us go in the next room."

In the next room, Aleyevtsev continued:

"I will designate you provincial secretary, which means you will receive a rank."

The document was written, but, to Dobrynin's horror, it was placed under cloth.

"But why?" he uttered.

"Gavriil Ivanovich, we need to find a time to sign it."

But the next day, Aleyevtsev began to drink, drink at home and drink himself unconscious.

The house was locked and a soldier named Danilka Cerberus

stood by the doors, although he had use of both his eyes.

Dobrynin knocked in vain and gave Danilka first a ruble, then another two.

Danilka was silent and his breath gave off the smell of onion and vodka in Dobrynin's face.

Only later did Gavriil find out that Danilka collected no less than twenty-five rubles; then it turned out that the snub-nosed provincial secretary Teplynin had erased Dobrynin's name from the roster and wrote in his own because it had not yet been signed by the governor. He inscribed Dobrynin's name in place of his own for the vacancy of steward to the governorate administration.

This would give him an inferior grade and a salary lower by sixty rubles.

He had to act decisively.

Dobrynin went to see Kakhovsky and heard him only say the words "Very well."

But Gavriil Ivanovich continued to bow and wouldn't leave.

Kakhovsky gazed at him attentively and added:

"Go to the Governor's chancery at ten o'clock and tell them on my behalf that the Governor was advised about you, and I will be there."

Dobrynin went out on the street and thought:

"Should I call on Mr. Vyazmitinov? After all, the sleds came with bears."

Vyazmitinov had just returned from visiting the Count in Polotsk and took lodgings in town.

Dobrynin entered without an announcement.

Vyazmitinov was sitting behind a table in full uniform stooped over his papers.

Gavriil Ivanovich took a bow and began to expound on his esteem and the regards sent by brother Ivan Kozmich.

The General-Adjutant stood up, walked to the middle of the room and asked quickly:

"When have you last seen him? Where are you serving? Why are you here?"

Dobrynin rattled off:

"I wish to obtain a rank and position on the basis of mercy rather than merit. I saw him two weeks ago, my name is Dobrynin, and I'm in an uncertain situation."

"Oh, the sleigh," the General-Adjutant remembered. "They even sent me your beer."

Just then, Kakhovsky walked in.

And, seeing that the supplicant was already speaking to the General-Adjutant, he said:

"What about, what about ten o'clock?"

At that moment, a Malorussian man with a large head and an ashen, freckled face walked in. He wore a toupee on his head that resembled a loose sail or a windmill's vanes. His braid was hidden in a hair net the color of dark cherry. His caftan was also cherry-colored with golden loops. And there was a chapeau bras under his left shoulder.

The man entered and began to speak in French rapidly.

"So that's what they're like, Parisians!" Dobrynin thought, recalling the Bishop.

But Vyazmitinov asked his guest in Russian:

"How did you like Mogilev, Mr. Polyansky?"

Dobrynin was admitted to the Governor's chancery without the ceremony of waiting in the foyer.

The Governor looked at Dobrynin in silence.

Colonel Kakhovsky gestured for Gavriil Ivanovich to step out.

The inspection was over.

In the chancery, Dobrynin was asked by a young governorate secretary:

"Where are those recommendations from the provincial chancery that Aleyevtsev had written to designate you as secretary, as you told Mr. Kakhovsky?"

"They're on this table, under the cloth," Dobrynin said, lifting the red felt.

The document was still in its place.

Kakhovsky came out an hour later and said:

"Congratulations on becoming a governorate secretary."

"Who are they saying this to?" the clerks asked each other in the chancery.

"To me!" Dobrynin said.

"Oh, brother, evidently, you don't have our troubles."

Dobrynin was no longer just an officer, but a headquarters officer.

At that moment, Mr. Kakhovsky came up to him and said:

"And that pug Secretary Teplynin, who had the foolish impudence to erase your name from the roster, was assigned to a chancery position under your command. You can scrape his hide a bit."

If it wasn't for his sword, Dobrynin would have fallen to Mr. Kakhovsky's feet, but his sword dug into the ground again and, the next moment, Polyansky walked out with his spry Parisian gait and said in Russian:

"Our new governorate secretary even has noble manners."

Thank you, sword!

Mr. Kakhovsky looked at Dobrynin with tenderness and said:

"Thank the Messrs. Vyazmitinov."

But the path to the stars was arduous.

A. Aleyevtsev—although he wasn't the one who introduced you or wrote it—and what if he cites or transfers or dismisses you?

The new governorate secretary ran down the streets of Mogilev. And here are the wooden pillars of Aleyevtsev's home, and here is the door.

The altar boy thought to himself:

Oh, the great Danilka, son of a blind and momentary chance, oh, loyal guard by the gates of the great clerk, oh powerful Cerberus, take pity on me!

Then, he said loudly:

"Listen, I was sent here with a note from Colonel Vasiliy Vasilyevich Kakhovsky. Here is a note from him, this note is the most important note there ever was from the beginning of all secretaries' gates and guards named Danilka."

And Dobrynin thrust a twenty-five-ruble banknote through the crevice instead of a note.

The door opened quietly.

Suddenly, the councilor to the chamber expedition Pyotr Ilyich Surmin squeezed in sideways through the same door.

But Danilka's firm elbow met Surmin. And Danilka's voice pronounced:

"I have not been instructed to admit you, sir."

But Surmin replied quick-wittedly:

"You, Danilka, don't know that you've been assigned to us in the governorate administration as a sentinel and I will crush you there."

And Danilka's hand descended.

Behind the foyer, behind the corridor, sat the drunk, but not too drunk, Aleyevtsev in his uniform, but without any trousers on.

"I'm glad," he said, "that you, Gavriil Ivanovich, have petitioned on your own behalf. You did the right thing by calling on me because I will register you not on May 17, when you came, but on April 30, because in May, the Governor's authority to distribute ranks had expired and, without my assistance, it would be as if you weren't given one."

At that moment, another fifty-ruble banknote began to inch across the table.

As he said this, Aleyevtsev examined governorate dossiers and, suddenly, perhaps for show, tore up one of the Governor's proposals.

Aleyevtsev raised his blue, drunken eyes and said:

"This is a dispute between the chamber expedition and the

Governor, and it would be better to spare Mikhail Vasilyevich. And now, take the recommendation to the Rogachev provincial chancery and ask them to write the following resolution: "Submit a request to the chamber expedition to collect a fee to be sent to the treasury in exchange for a rank." Then, it will look as if the document had been left for too long at the registry and your designation is lawful. And I won't assign you to the chamber expedition, but to the treasury chamber, the new people—the Parisian Polyansky himself."

Dobrynin's joy was almost of tremulous. But the next day, there was an incident.

A letter from Vyazmitinov came stating that he didn't know why Dobrynin wasn't returning to his post. It was a delicate matter because Dobrynin had already exploited Vyazmitinov's name.

He was obliged to go to Rogachev. It turned out that Vyazmitinov was not too thrilled about Dobrynin's new galloons.

He was forced to squeeze a little bit more oil out of himself. The amount he paid is unknown.

But another letter from Aleyevtsev came requesting that the commissariat chancery clerk Mr. Dobrynin be sent to serve at the treasury chamber.

Dobrynin rode out at night and looked at the stars all along the way.

On the Parisian Mr. Polyansky

THE TOWN OF Mogilev was not small. There was Mr. Gamaley, the chancery administrator and a famous Freemason, but his story will not fit in this book; the first Governor was Count Chernyshev and, after him, Mr. Passek, while the Bishop was Georgiy Konissky.

We will discuss Konissky later; first, let us consider Passek.

Passek was among those gentlemen-at-arms who, on a hazy day, had installed Catherine on the Russian throne.

Like a true guardsman, Passek was tall. His name was Pyotr Bogdanovich.

He was considered one of the leaders of the plot. They tried to arrest him, and the coup began as a result of that arrest. On account of the coup, he received the title of Captain of the Guard, twenty-four thousand rubles, a village just outside of Moscow and a farm in Revel, and the following year, an additional four thousand rubles and an annuity of one thousand.

He was the Governor of the Mogilev governorate and, in 1771, replaced Count Chernyshev as the Governor-General of Belarus.

It was under his command that Mr. Polyansky came to flourish.

Polyansky, who came from Kazan gentry, served in Siberia and was distinguished for his diligence; in 1771, while living in Switzerland with a view to bettering his education, he became friends with Voltaire.

He was one of those Russians who were enamored with the Parisian Arc de Triomphe.

Voltaire was personally fond of him and wrote letters about him to the serene Catherine:

". . . At present, there is a subject of yours in my desert, a Mr. Polyansky, a native of your Kazan kingdom. I cannot praise him enough for his courtesy, prudence, and gratitude for Your Imperial Majesty's favors."

In the second letter, dated December 3:

". . . Mr. Polyansky sometimes honors me with his presence. He enraptures us with his description of the grandeur of your court, your clemency, your tireless exertions, and the myriad great projects that you carry out in jest, so to speak. In a word, he drives me to despair because I am almost ninety years old and may not observe any of this for myself. Mr. Polyansky has a prodigious desire to see Italy, where he would learn more about serving your Imperial Majesty than in the neighboring Switzerland and Geneva. As intelligent as he is, he is also a very kind man whose heart is devoted to Your Majesty with true zeal."

Whereupon the Empress replied:

". . . I ordered to expedite to Mr. Polyansky, whom you have taken under your patronage, the funds necessary for his journey to Italy, and believe that he has received them at this very hour."

In the third letter, dated December 11, 1772, Voltaire wrote:

". . . I received the sad news that the same Polyansky who, at your discretion, was traveling and whom I loved and admired immeasurably, had drowned in the Neva upon his return to St. Petersburg. If this is true, then I regret it exceedingly. Private misfortunes will always take place, but you ensure overall prosperity."

And in the fourth letter, dated January 3, 1773:

". . . Mr. Polyansky informs me that he has not drowned as I was told, that, on the contrary, he is in a quiet refuge and that Your Majesty has made him Secretary of the Academy."

That was Polyansky.

Mr. Polyansky didn't drown, but did have various adventures.

He had an amorous escapade in Moscow and abducted someone else's—Mr. Demidov's—wife in his coach, fighting off the police on his tail with his sword, and for that, and also for his insolent answers, Mr. Polyansky was sentenced by the Senate to have his most-impudent right hand chopped off.

But, at the time, Catherine the Empress was, provisionally, still a young woman, much like all the officials in Mogilev were acting officials, and this seemed to the most-gracious Empress a lighthearted case of chivalry, so she pardoned Polyansky.

Count Chernyshev requested Polyansky for the governorate administration, assuring Her Majesty that when he was young, he was just as enterprising.

The governorate was already growing older, the porters' liveries had worn out and the copper maces had faded, but Polyansky continued to flourish under Chernyshev and under Passek.

Passek was only interested in horses, his lover, and his illegitimate son.

Whereas Polyansky was ambitious.

His knowledge of languages, literature, dances, and cards, as well as his quick wit and propitious memory made Polyansky somewhat of a dictator in the governorate.

He placed insolent and stupid nobles under arrest and sent incorrigible secretaries and servants there too; he didn't waste words on the commoners and simply ordered them to obey him in silence.

Many tried to start an argument with Polyansky, but he always came out the winner.

And he was the most important person in all the governorate, though he was only two arshins and two vershoks tall in heels.

The 1779 passage of the Empress Catherine, who was also known as the sun, was a remarkable year for Mogilev. She drove through town in the month of May to board the galleys and continue via the Dnieper as far as Kherson, surveying the establishments of the newly acquired governorates. In May, the divine Catherine proceeded through Mogilev and with her came, under the name of Count Falkenstein, the Austrian and Holy Roman Emperor Joseph II. He was traveling incognito and arrived in Mogilev a day before the Empress.

He was of medium height and had a Germanic complexion— that is to say, a ruddy one rather than a white one.

He walked around in a green garrison uniform and would not have attracted attention had Governor Passek not bowed to him too low.

In the evening, in the Mogilev Bishop's garden, the Emperor

spoke with Count Potemkin.

Dobrynin walked around the town ramparts, from which he could see everything in the garden.

More than anything, the Emperor resembled a carpenter or a bookbinder. Potemkin, a large man of robust constitution but a bit portly, had only one eye, but this didn't seem to spoil his face. He stood there speaking to the Emperor; neither of them wore hats; an orderly held Potemkin's hat, which was spangled with precious stones and appeared heavy.

The Emperor held his own hat and was keenly engaged in conversation with Potemkin.

Potemkin yawned, bit his nails, and was visibly bored.

Dobrynin was all eyes.

"There he is, the seminarian from Smolensk who received a medal at the Moscow University, the interlocutor of Zaikonospassky monks. He, the happy rival of Orlov. Only recently a sergeant-major and now a Prince, the famous vanquisher of the Ottoman Porta, a Prince of the Holy Roman Empire, the founder of Kherson, the head of the Order of the Holy Great Prince Vladimir, Equal of the Apostles, the Colonel-in-Chief of the Chevalier Guards, and a knight of all the orders crowned with a laurel wreath strewn with emeralds and diamonds by the Empress herself and, in addition to all that, a commander of the Zaporozhian Cossacks and Black Sea troops.

"There he is yawning and biting his nails."

At night, Dobrynin couldn't sleep, and the rank of governorate secretary seemed to him rather low.

Oh, glory!

Her Majesty arrived in town with a convoy of the Cuirassier Regiment. She rode through the triumphal arches erected for the occasion. In the cathedral, the Empress was welcomed by the clergy, and Georgiy Konissky pronounced his famous speech.

The speech was so bombastic that the renowned hierarch himself stood on his tiptoes.

I will not cite this speech in full, but will provide an excerpt from its beginning:

"Let the astronomers judge if the sun revolves around us or if we revolve around it along with the Earth. Our sun revolves around us. The wisest monarch departs like a groom leaving his hall. Your passage extends from the end of the Baltic Sea to the end of the Black Sea and no one can hide from the boons of your warmth. Alas, our sun is in a hurry! Traveling with Cyclopean footsteps; our only hope is that your life isn't in a hurry westward; otherwise, we will cling to you and demand like Joshua the Son of Nun: stand still, sun, and don't move, until you have vanquished all who oppose your intentions."

This sun had a slightly doughy and squat appearance. At first, it bowed to the ground, then it grew weary and sat down in its seat, which was expressly prepared for the occasion.

The seat was sectioned off, and devotees didn't even see that the sun, which sighed piously, was calmly playing solitaire.

As for Georgiy Konissky, he received a cross with diamonds for this speech. And Passek received an entire jewel box with snuffboxes, watches, and rings to distribute to the people. But the former Royal Guardsman's finances were so poor that he decided not to distribute the items.

Then, they laid the foundation stone of St. Joseph's church, and here, Georgiy Konissky gave the speech again and the Empress replied to him briefly and inattentively.

It was also here that many representatives of the Belarus gentry were given Russian ranks.

And many of those retitled didn't understand why they don't have regiments if they are named colonels.

Catherine had less use for Georgiy Konissky than she did for the szlachta, which is why she greeted the old bishop aloofly.

They had to reconcile with the nobility to promote the

universal order of the Empire, which, at the time, rested entirely on the gentry.

As for the Eastern Orthodox Christians, they were peasants. And it was premature to convert Uniates to Orthodox Christianity.

The governorate chancery teemed with the szlachta, who were asking what a titular councilor and what a court councilor were.

The officials snarled at these questions because they didn't have their own titles yet.

At last, the Empress departed to the sound of ringing bells.

Only nervous and curious Jews watched her departure.

The Belarusians regarded the passage of the Empress and the Holy Roman Emperor with indifference. Catherine's sun burned rather than warmed them.

Mr. Polyansky and Gavriil Ivanovich Dobrynin live next to each other

POLYANSKY DROVE AROUND the entire governorate asking questions, writing everything down, and taking soil samples. Soon, he was familiar with all of the boggy, wooded Belarus.

He loved to brag about his knowledge and, going as far as inquiring about some landowner in advance, was fond of dumbfounding the latter, calling him directly by his name and patronymic.

But all this seemed like an empty farce to Dobrynin and even reminded him of the behavior of monastery hermits, who, through their servants, found out various details about the higher-ranked devotees in order to dazzle them with their clairvoyance.

Dobrynin knew that when his predecessor left the governorate administration, he placed fifty thousand rubles for Vitebsk

Jesuits in the secure loan institution.

All this time, he was looking to set upon and apply himself to something, but he didn't know what or how.

It turned out that he should apply himself to mast timber.

They chopped down State-owned wood under the pretense that it was landowners' wood and drifted it down the Dvina River to Riga, and from Riga, abroad.

Timber was a sought-after commodity and all the timber in Riga had been sold for many years in advance.

Dobrynin inspected the laws on this matter; there were as many as six pages listing the titles of these laws in the legal handbook.

Then, Mr. Dobrynin understood that there was a chance to make a fortune at this.

It turned out that the wood also extended in the other direction and it also turned out that His Serene Highness Prince Potemkin gave Governor-General Passek two thousand tithes of oakwood not far from the Mayak settlement, which had been owned by the State since the time of Peter the Great.

This settlement is located between Bakhmut and Taganrog and there's no other wood in the 200-verst radius.

This wood was a sanctuary and expensive; Passek didn't have any titles to this wood except for a private letter from Potemkin.

They were building a fleet on the Black Sea and a wood—particularly someone else's—was fitting for this; they needed to chop rapidly.

Dobrynin traveled to Taganrog on an errand from Passek and saw that there was a lot of snow, no firewood, that they burned reeds for heat, that the caviar was cheap, and that there wasn't a lot of water.

But it was difficult to sell this timber without any documents. In any case, a brave man turned up and bought the sanctuary, which was worth at least 100,000 rubles, for 35,000.

He had to hurry.

Potemkin and the Empress herself were both mortal. And it was still unknown what the future Emperor Pavel Petrovich would say about selling State-owned wood.

As for Polyansky, he was absolutely flourishing and didn't get involved in any dubious schemes, but introduced a so-called European administration system to the governorate. In his leisure, he pursued the arts.

There was an amateur theater in town where a young woman by the name of von Brink, who was already twenty-four, played the heroines.

Polyansky frequented the theater and relished explaining to the maiden von Brink, in the French dialect, the ideas of the illustrious Diderot, who stated that the actor must not possess the feelings he is trying to portray on stage.

"Hence," Mr. Polyansky said, "you with your, without exaggeration, sensitive and boundless soul, cannot portray a heroine or a lover because you have those feelings in your soul. A naturally occurring diamond cannot depict paste."

The young woman listened.

It isn't exactly known if they did anything else besides talk.

There was also a General von Brink in town, a relative of the maiden von Brink.

This General was known around town for his slovenliness.

Boys ran after him and yelled out verses with rich rhymes.

"General, General . . . soiled!"

And what it was that he soiled was inserted according to the wishes of the teasing boy.

And, suddenly, the old Lady von Brink summoned her relative and proposed that he marry the beautiful amateur actress.

The marriage took place.

At the time, Mr. Polyansky was thirty-eight. He was of unconventional character. And always fell in love with others' wives. At present, Lady von Brink seemed doubly charming to him.

He walked around the chancery and recited poems well-known to Dobrynin:

Love grows out of obstacles and fear
And, flung to extremities, dares anything there is.

Dobrynin, who was by now a titular councilor, and able to sell woods all along the Dvina and the Dnieper, valued Polyansky's opinion and interrupted him warmly with the words:

"I believe this poem is by the famous Mr. Sumarokov?"

"Yes," Polyansky answered. "You, Gavriil Ivanovich, are an educated man."

And again, he repeated those verses, and this sometimes happened up to ten times a day.

The entire town waited for what would happen next. Only Mr. von Brink was calm. However, his friend, the Lieutenant Baron Felich, was concerned; he was very fond of the General and was convinced that the General possessed every possible virtue and even youth, although the General was well over fifty.

Polyansky rented an apartment in the pastor's home across from the one where Mr. von Brink lived. Consequently, the lover and the husband were separated by a single street called Wayward Street.

One beautiful morning, when the sparrows were chirping as they're doing now, Mr. von Brink woke up.

Von Brink woke up and asked: "Where is my wife?"

He was told: "We don't know."

The General sat down to drink coffee. He drank it leisurely for two hours.

He asked again: "Where is my wife?"

They replied with embarrassment that his wife went out to see the pastor.

"At this hour?" the General said. "What is this about praying! Tell her to come to the pavilion to drink coffee and, if she doesn't want coffee, then hot chocolate."

"She left for good and is living at the pastor's."

"What do you mean, living? There isn't even space!"

"There was an empty space there, Your Excellency, they cleaned it three days ago and covered the floor with cloth. And now, the furniture in that house is arranged in perfect symmetry."

"Symmetry," the General repeated. "I will go look at the symmetry."

He was befuddled. During one skirmish at Ochakov's house, he had been hit by a slingshot, which were supplied to Russian troops at the time.

The servants explained compassionately that it was impossible to go have a look at the General's wife because there was a sentry from the governorate administration at her doors.

The General was surprised:

"Has she really been arrested?"

There was a sudden knock on the door and the headquarters doctor Avraam Vasilyevich Bychkov walked in with his attendants and the police.

Bychkov was slightly embarrassed and the police, given their rank's intrinsically coarse nature, were sniggering.

"We received," the physician said, "a petition from the wife of the General von Brink, born von Brink, stating that her husband is unfit for married life and that she, therefore, requests the governorate administration to conduct a medical inspection so as to commence divorce proceedings."

Baron Felich, the General's friend, took the order in his hands.

It was signed by Polyansky.

"This is knavery," the Baron said.

The General was perplexed.

"But how could all this happen? My wife is at the pastor's house, the furniture is arranged symmetrically there, her petition is signed, a resolution is ready, you have an order and wish to examine me. And all this while I was drinking coffee."

The headquarters doctor replied politely:

"Take off your clothes, Your Excellency, we will examine you, after which the General's wife will either obtain the right to hide under the roof of the pastor's respectable house or will return to your arms."

At that moment, the General lost his temper:

"I am a Major-General and a Knight of the Order of St. George and, moreover, my own barber Geissler has three children and they're by me and you know it! Günther, what is your papa's name? Show us your papa!"

A boy of three ran in.

"Günther, show Papa," the General repeated.

"Good morning, Papa," the boy answered. "You have forbidden me to point to you."

The boy, dirty and three years of age, wasn't sufficient proof.

"I ask you to undress," Bychkov insisted.

Then, the General took a short rifle off the wall and said:

"Messieurs, I will now butcher you with this rifle butt."

Seeing this, the doctor and police retreated.

It was as if the proceeding came to an end.

The General lived on one side of Wayward Street and the General's wife lived on the other, and Polyansky went to call on the pastor.

The prosperous and tranquil existence of Gavriil Ivanovich Dobrynin

TRUTH BE TOLD, in exchange for the State-owned mast wood sent down the Dvina River in the guise of landowners' wood, Dobrynin received only a quarter of the bribe, precisely twenty gold coins and, later, an additional seventy-five rubles in banknotes. Truth be told, Mr. Passek's commission on the sale of State-owned woods ran into trouble; however, the vodka venture was successful.

Vodka played a political role in the governorate in general.

In the vodka trade, the old nobility competed with the newly appointed noble bureaucrats, who weren't entitled to sell vodka under the rather widespread law of 1765.

The Jews competed with the nobility in vodka, or, rather, the sale of it, and Mr. Passek even proposed to banish all Jews in view of their unscrupulous competition with the nobles.

Dobrynin himself didn't sell vodka, recalling the sixth provision of the ordinance of 1765:

"Persons who are not issued from nobility and possess officers' ranks in the service are not permitted by law to profit from noblemen's rights; after their first illicit sale of alcohol, such persons shall be deprived of their rank and excluded from service and, after the second, sent to a mountain labor colony."

But there was a finer business.

And less risky.

It was permitted under law to manufacture French vodka, that is to say, vodka distilled from fruit or grapes.

Manufacturers of such vodka were obliged to supply it to a State chamber for medical trials and the chamber was obliged to affix a stamp on every bottle after collecting a toll.

There was in Belarus a Mr. Augsburg, a German count, an Italian subject, and a Belarusian resident.

He presented some vodkas for trial—his vodkas were yellow, green, white, liqueur, and punch.

The vodkas had not only already been sent to the chamber, but to every official's residence.

There was an antiquated caricature.

The Austrian emperor is eating Holland, which is represented by a cheese, and the Prussian king looks over his shoulder and says, "I like Dutch cheese too."

Dobrynin liked all kinds of cheese, but they didn't even send him any vodka. But on the beautiful morning when the sparrows were chirping and the recipient of the Order of St. George General von Brink was marveling, the solicitor Tselikovsky came to see Gavriil Ivanovich.

"It is possible to do business," he said, "with vodka."

"But how? It has already been issued."

"One may have been issued, but the other one hasn't and is being stamped outside town gates, in Mr. Golynsky's empty house."

"Let us consult the law."

In the index to the legal handbook, close to four pages were dedicated to ordinances related to vodka and wine, starting on page sixty-five.

The ordinance dated December 28, 1766 was the most suitable. After reading it, Dobrynin had a flash of inspiration and said:

"Why not in a State chamber? Have they made the new seal mandated by law? Just how many bottles are being stamped? Is it possible to stamp five thousand bottles outside of town instead of one thousand?"

"Mr. Dobrynin," Tselikovsky said, "we should discuss this, but not in a State chamber; let us go outside town gates, to Golynsky's house."

Things moved quickly; the replicated seal and the vodka stamped with that seal were hunted down outside of town, but it was difficult to advance the inquiry any further.

The prosecutor refused to listen to them and the protocol vanished.

But at the treasury, they managed to find out that the toll—ten kopecks per bottle—had never been received.

And it turned out that the stamped vodka had not been distilled from fruit, but from grain, and that the Governor-General had not been paid off either.

And the seal, though it appeared genuine, wasn't wholly authentic.

Thus, the following order arrived:

"Hereby declaring the omission made in this regard, I submit to the governorate administration the report of the provincial prosecutor and solicitors, who have conducted inspections with the assistance of medical staff residing in Mogilev, and advise them to proceed in accordance with the law and henceforth carry out the stamping of the aforesaid vodka on the premises of the State chamber, designating one hundred to five hundred bottles of the aforesaid vodka daily for stamping so as to prevent crammed quarters and the wasting of bottles, assigning a military sentinel to it for as long as the aforesaid shall continue to be stamped, and, this time around, informing the solicitor and all medical staff residing in town of any State concerns; finally, I deem it necessary to inspect that their vodka is distilled solely from grape wine and grape berries pursuant to the aforesaid mandates."

Following this order, the vodka was, of course, not made from grape wine, but the Count was still obliged to add grape wine to it. As for Dobrynin, he received continuous access to this trade and a simultaneous annual tribute of three hundred and sixty rubles from the Count.

Meanwhile, what was Mr. von Brink doing?

The continuation of Mr. Polyansky's adventures

LOVE THRIVED IN the pastor's house.

Polyansky spent almost whole days there, but governorate affairs occasionally required that he leave for at least a few hours.

Deeply sighing, the Parisian would leave the theater where the feelings were real.

And to alleviate boredom at the governorate bureau, he

appointed a courier who carried endless love notes between the pastor's house and the governorate palace.

Baron Felich intercepted one such note for a future court case and Mr. Polyansky, with a decisiveness that was outright gubernatorial, arrested the pastor's child at the chancery.

Then, the pastor and the pastor's wife turned to the Governor, but the Governor couldn't do anything about Polyansky.

Suddenly, an astounding event took place.

The pastor and the pastor's wife ran through town shouting, entered the governorate administration chancery, took their son, and brought him home without any written mandate.

And Polyansky didn't say anything, not being able to bring himself to initiate legal proceedings against the pastor.

This was surprising to the town population.

Presently, not only did this undermine Polyansky's glory, but the pastor's house, the nest of the Parisian gentleman's happiness, became a house of dispute.

But then, a consolatory parcel arrived from St. Petersburg.

It turned out that the divorce case was advancing and that Lady von Brink would soon be known as maiden von Brink because she had decided to undergo a medical inspection herself.

The happy and satisfied Polyansky was traveling with a servant to an audit in the Chernigov district.

All of a sudden, he came upon the Lieutenant Baron Felich and two other unidentified men in the woods.

Baron Felich began to shout:

"Oh, hero of Mogilev, you're not in the Senate here!"

Polyansky replied from his carriage:

"Baron, it would be dishonest of you to exact revenge. Do it the European way: you take a pistol, I'll take another, and these unknown noblemen will be our seconds."

But the Baron was drunk and merry.

"In Europe," he said, "they don't send a doctor and police officers to the husband's house for a medical inspection."

Then, they grabbed Polyansky and began to whip him.

Peasants found Polyansky abandoned in the woods and brought him to Mogilev.

All of Mogilev visited Polyansky the hero. Georgiy Konissky himself called on him with a comforting sermon. Dobrynin came with Lutsevin. They were admitted directly after the doctor and wrote a complaint against Felich and Brink.

However, at the governorate administration, the presiding officer rejected the complaint for having been written in invective.

One denunciation followed another. Akhsharumov wrote one against Polyansky and Polyansky wrote one against Akhsharumov.

General von Brink sold his house, then his uniform, and the rest was taken by higher justice.

The old man became a street beggar. And if anyone gave him alms, he would stop the benefactor and say:

"I still don't understand: why did Baron von Felich fight with Polyansky over my wife, what does the Governor-General have to do with all this, and why don't I have a place to drink coffee now? Why did I take pity on my poor relative, why did I cover another's sin with my name?"

Then, Mr. von Brink would start to cry and ask for money for tobacco. All this was very unpleasant and people tried to avoid him.

Mr. Dobrynin prospers

ONE TIME, MR. DOBRYNIN was summoned by none other than the Governor-General.

The Governor-General received him affectionately and even said:

"Sit down."

Gavriil Ivanovich sat down and gazed with pleasure in the large gubernatorial mirror.

There weren't many of these in Mogilev.

In the mirror, on the gilded, velvet-cushioned chair glazed with white enamel, sat a young man of thirty-four, as far as Dobrynin knew. The man was well dressed in a gray silk caftan and matching stockings. Moreover, the man had a sword and was sitting with Governor-General Passek in the flesh.

The mirror showed a very pleasant sight.

And it was even pleasant to think that, although Kirill of Sevsk hadn't been banished to the Suzdal and Solovetsky monastery and wasn't sitting in a dungeon chasing away rats with a stick, he had, nevertheless, been presently removed from his position and received an annuity of only three hundred rubles, having been sent to a monastery he couldn't even run.

And what monastery—the Kiev-Mikhailovsky, a poor one.

Whereas Gavriil Ivanovich Dobrynin sat with the Governor and had money growing at quadruple interest.

They paid him for vodka, they paid him for timber, there was no dossier in his name at the Senate, and he hadn't been whipped anywhere.

In his jubilation, Gavriil Ivanovich didn't observe that the Governor was a bit embarrassed.

Yes, Pyotr Bogdanovich, a Senator and a Knight of the Order of St. Andrew the First-Called, which was a rare order, was embarrassed.

He began somewhat uneasily:

"My friend, I had a brother named Vasiliy and this brother was in love with our first cousin Yelizaveta Ilyinichna Obrutskaya. And, under the rules of our holy Orthodox church, he couldn't marry her. So what did my poor brother do? He advised my poor first cousin to leave her dress on the riverbank when she went swimming and then leave town. As it were, we thought Yelizaveta Ilyinichna had drowned while she, using the name

Nadezhda Petrovna, had gone to a Ukrainian estate and illegally married my brother, which was witnessed by . . ."

Gavriil Ivanovich sat composed and no longer looked in the mirror, but at the Governor-General.

The latter was embarrassed and continued confusedly:

"I was present there and signed as a witness because I loved my brother very much. But, after all," the General continued, "the marriage is unlawful. My brother died, and, in his will, he left his fortune to his son, whom he had begotten with our first cousin; the son's name is Vasiliy and the executor was Count Gendrikov, but now that the Count is dead, I am the executor."

"Very amusing!" Dobrynin exclaimed.

The Governor-General cast an embarrassed glance and continued:

"In memory of my heroism during her ascension to the throne, the Empress paid my debts a few times. But even now, I am hopelessly in debt and . . ."

At this time, Gavriil Ivanovich began to speak:

"You do not wish to leave the estate to your nephew and consider him illegitimate?"

"Yes, I don't, I have my own children, although they, too, are illegitimate; but they are my children. I must," Passek continued, "initiate a proceeding to dissolve the marriage—you cannot cover incest with a nuptial crown. Thus, I summoned you as a man of law and was also told that you are an expert in chancery matters."

Gavriil Ivanovich was already slouching in his seat.

"Of course," he said, "Your Excellency is absolutely right. The marriage is unlawful. But when the action is commenced, the marriage witnesses will be summoned and the Senator and Knight of all orders Pyotr Bogdanovich Passek will be brought before the court. Moreover, the canons have substitutes for highly ranked persons. Our sovereign, the mother of our homeland Catherine, was closely related by marriage and by blood to her husband Peter III, and, under stringent law, the marriage was, so to speak, invalid; and the late Empress Elizabeth Petrovna was born out of wedlock and only crowned in marriage."

"Hush!" Passek said.

"Do not fret, we are speaking in secret."

At that moment, Dobrynin lowered his voice:

"There was a plan, Your Excellency, to marry Elizabeth Petrovna to her nephew Ioann Antonovich to end the claims of the Brunswick family. Her Majesty the Empress can change the canon herself and the case will reach her. I know that Vasiliy Bogdanovich, your brother, was a friend of the Generalissimo Suvorov, and it is uncertain who will be judge if the case goes to trial and what they'll decide. It is a petty and expensive case."

"What do you advise me to do?"

"Your Excellency, I would record your illegitimate nephew Vasiliy Vasilyevich as Laskovyy rather than Passek in all the books, with a spelling error, so to speak. And, for now, pay out his money directly to him. If a dispute arises, all his documents will appear rather suspicious."

"Do as you wish, nettle seed," said the Governor-General. "And be gone from here!"

"Your Excellency," said Dobrynin, "I've been made officer four times and would like to, at present, be awarded the rank of collegiate assessor."

"You will be. Now go and do as you said."

The holy man blooms like a date palm

THE COLLEGIATE ASSESSOR and recipient of the Order of St. Anna Gavriil Dobrynin was thriving.

His circumstances were improving, he had already bought himself a house in Mogilev.

The house wasn't too big, but suitable: on the edge of town, four and a half by four sazhens, four rooms downstairs and a fifth one upstairs. The outhouse was in the courtyard.

The furniture inside was as it should be; Dobrynin himself had a sky-blue fur coat with a dark-brown fox fur collar.

The house was surrounded by a garden, and in the garden there were flowers and apple trees blooming as they once did at the monastery, and even roses.

In the courtyard, various banisters had been built with planks to enclose places unpleasant to sight and smell.

The roof was green, the fence was blue, and there was an inscription on the gates:

"Relieved from quartering soldiers."

It was nice to sit in a house like this and ponder that Aleyevtsev drank himself to death, Shpynev died of dropsy, and Gorchakov vanished.

While he, Dobrynin, sits and sips a fashionable tea from a cubic samovar with a clawfoot stand.

While the passersby smell the roses and ask each other:

"And whose beautiful house is this?"

And the caretaker replies:

"It belongs to His Honor the collegiate assessor Gavriil Ivanovich Dobrynin."

Only, from time to time, the passersby say:

"Oh, that one, the priest's son . . ."

Then, the young Dobrynin stands up and, feeling Fliorinsky's blood in him, yells across the fence:

"You're a priest's son, son of a bitch!"

Good manners are always rewarded this way.

Polyansky is ill, he cannot stand up, they walk with him arm-in-arm, although he is still involved in the divorce proceedings.

Polyansky had a friend, the councilor Surmin, a quiet family man, but not trim or concerned with his health, and that man also fell ill.

One time, Dobrynin was at Surmin's house—that clever mind could still prove useful.

The servants announced:

"Mr. Polyansky's coach has arrived."

The host was pleased to see the guest, he went out in the great hall in his housecoat, leaning on a crutch; he was met halfway by Polyansky, his old friend, beaten, ill, and also on crutches. They were both held up by the footmen.

Surmin was quiet but intelligent, had read both Voltaire's books and Russian books and loved Fonvizin's atheist message to his servants.

Polyansky looked at him, twisted his mouth, and, suddenly, they both began to roar with laughter with all that remained of their strength.

Then, they sat on the sofa and the servants laid pillows before them; the friends looked at each other once more, burst into laughter, and then began to cry.

"Well," said Surmin, "how's the divorce?"

"The divorce will come through soon," Polyansky said. "Von Brink has already been taken to Riga, he was brought before the court and I feel sorry for him."

And Polyansky burst into laughter again.

As for Dobrynin, he stood up, bowed politely, and waved his hat like his hero the Bachelor Don Cherubim de la Ronda, and went home to drink evening tea under the lilacs.

Because a holy man blooms like a date tree.

Once more on serving the Bishop

DOBRYNIN LED A quiet, splendidly quiet life in Mogilev.

He developed official relations with his lover, the Governor-General's wife Saltykova.

Maria Sergeyevna gave him the power of attorney for the administration and sale of the estate.

His was a house of plenty.

In the evenings, Dobrynin read books and the newspaper to which he subscribed, *The Moscow Journal*.

He read which ships had arrived, he read that the Swiss king traveled to Ludwigslust and awaited his coach on the road.

He read advertisements for houses being sold in Moscow, for horses, and for books.

More and more books were being published.

The Empire was prospering, so to speak.

People were going up in price too. A good barber could charge as much as a thousand or twelve hundred rubles.

The only surprising news came out of Paris.

The news was peculiar; it was no longer the same Paris where the Bishop Kirill had dreamt of riding sturgeons.

It appeared in the newspaper that, in Spain, it was forbidden to even speak about France.

It was a midsummer July evening.

The sun had already set.

A round, poorly polished moon resembling a worn-out silver-plated church dish dangled from the sky.

It was a Saturday and bells rang over Mogilev.

The shops were closed.

Gavriil Ivanovich entered the cathedral.

Divine service hadn't begun yet, but the cathedral was pleasantly cool.

The choirboys took their places in the choir gallery, clearing their throats.

Someone struck Gavriil Ivanovich on the shoulder. Without turning, Dobrynin stretched out his hand, thinking he was being asked to pass down a candle.

But Tselikovsky's familiar voice pronounced softly:

"Kirill of Sevsk is here."

"Whereabouts?"

"We saw him enter the altar with our Bishop."

Suddenly, the main doors in the middle of the altar, which were known as the Royal Gates, opened.

And wearing light garments with a pastor's staff in hand, none other than Fliorinsky came out on the pulpit.

The church was almost empty—no one was interested in seeing the undistinguished Bishop's service.

Kirill tried to impart a firmness and vigor to his steps and to assume a lofty posture.

But his legs dragged and his voice was dull.

The choirboys didn't sing very loudly, as if they were afraid of disturbing the tall, gaunt saints painted on the cathedral walls.

Four evangelists with four beasts—a singing, a howling, an invoking, and a jabbering one—were watching from the sails of the dome.

It was quiet behind the altar screen.

Dobrynin felt pity in his heart.

"Alas," he thought, "what happened to Kirill's verve and dexterity? And he isn't scolding anyone before the entire church or singeing any beards with candles here. It is now quiet behind the altar screen."

"This is what a twelve-year sentence does to a man in old age!"

Thus thought Gavriil, joining in the singing with his still-vigorous choirboy's voice to somehow magnify the solemnity of the service.

After the litany, Dobrynin paid a visit to the Bishop at the altar.

At the altar sat an already feeble old man; the Bishop wore a hare-fur mitten on his right hand despite it being a summer day.

Kirill gave his benediction and said:

"Tell me the truth: are you happy to see me?"

"Why wouldn't I be happy to see Your Grace, and in good health to boot? I pray that you come sup with me this evening."

"My health is not up to par, but I can call on you. I'm

traveling from my monastery to Moscow to receive medical treatment, and stopped in Mogilev to speak with your Bishop Georgiy Konissky. He was a teacher of mine in Kiev, but, in all honesty, I mainly came to have a look at you. Also, I need to see the Metropolitan Platon in Moscow. He is angry with me and I must make peace with him. When I return from Moscow, I will pass through Oryol, Sevsk, and Kiev. That is the circumference of my travels."

"These travels will strengthen Your Grace's health still more."

"I hope to God they will."

"What did Your Grace think of the Belarusian roads?"

"These roads are more like garden alleys. I think they must have cost much labor and sweat to the local residents."

"Nevertheless, their usefulness to travelers is unsurpassed."

Meanwhile, the devotees had already dispersed from the church.

The cathedral grew quiet and resonant.

Georgiy Konissky lit a candle and began to read prayers from the book, as was the custom at that hour for those who prepared the next day's service.

Kirill of Sevsk looked at Georgiy Konissky's bowed gray head with a smile and said:

"Gavriil, I see that this little man has been reading the prayers for the past forty years and could have known them by heart, and does know them by heart, but, behold! He has lit a candle—he fears that, without a candle, I won't see His Holiness."

The moon clambered up to the pinnacle of the sky.

Roses bloomed in the garden and the windows opened onto the garden.

Kirill wasn't late to supper.

The table was covered with genuine fruit vodkas: white ones, red ones, green ones, blue ones, punch ones, and liqueur ones.

Kirill sat down in the armchair and asked:

"So you never did marry?"

"There are no brides here, the Polish ones don't have dowries."

"You can amass your own dowry."

"I will marry when I amass it."

The candles were burning, the moon was beaming.

At present, Gavriil Ivanovich didn't fear the moon: it seemed that Kirill of Sevsk was no longer affected by either the new moon or the full moon.

"Do you have the ring again?"

The diamond ring that Gavriil had at one time returned was indeed gleaming on his finger.

"Naturally, in memory of Your Grace."

"Listen, do you know that your mother died?"

"Of course, I heard! What kind of vodka shall I pour you, Your Grace? We have fine vodkas, they are made by Count Augsburg, an Italian by birth, of German extraction and a Belasrusian resident."

"Yes. I sold my ring. Gavriil, they're clamping down on me at the monastery. They make me pay for everything and demand contributions. If I don't pay, I'll run into trouble."

Dobrynin was bored.

"Listen, Absalom," Kirill said, "light another candle, I'd like to have a look at your face."

They brought in candles. The shadows of the supping men quintupled on the walls.

"You're living well," Kirill said. "Your candles are plated and you've achieved everything at an early age like Gil Blas; only you haven't married, but you've achieved everything; what's next? But I want to reveal a certain secret to you."

"No secrets, Your Grace, I'm afraid of Mrs. Radcliffe and enjoy reading Sterne's sentimental books."

"Don't joke, Gavriil, you know . . ."

Gavriil Ivanovich stood up to put an end to the conversation, lowered his hand into his pocket, and took out a round silver snuffbox.

The snuffbox depicted some sort of an almost faded religious scene with Abraham sacrificing Isaac and God saying from a cloud: "Don't do it, I was only joking."

Kirill drank sweet vodka and wrinkled his face.

Gavriil Ivanovich unscrewed the snuffbox and there, carved on the ivory, was a gallant scene showing a monk openly dallying with a nun.

"Is it worthwhile to talk about such mysteries?" Gavriil uttered.

Kirill of Sevsk stood up and tried to strike Gavriil with his hare-mitten-covered hand.

"It isn't worthwhile," he said, and directed himself toward the door.

Gavriil followed him to the very gates; an old buggy stood by the gates and small horses were tangled in it like sheep. A monk sat in the coachman's seat, angry and scrawny.

When the Bishop came out, the monk didn't turn around.

The horses didn't set off right away, the buggy began to clatter.

The Bishop sat like a statue without turning around.

Then he said dully:

"Do you recall Anatoliy Meles? He died as well."

Gavriil took out the snuffbox again, smelled the tobacco, and raised his eyes. The buggy was already disappearing around the corner.

High in the sky dangled a round moon as faded as the snuffbox.

Dobrynin smiled, turned around as he held his sword, and walked spryly into his house. He sat down and opened a newspaper.

He was comforted to know that even in Moscow, prices weren't high. Beef fillets cost three and a half kopecks a pound and the rear parts cost three and a half and two and a half kopecks.

Beef fat was more expensive—six kopecks a pound, but it was intended for export.

It was rather expensive, but tolerably so.

Gavriil Ivanovich Dobrynin the collegiate assessor was attentively reading the newspaper.

He began on the back page because he was looking to purchase a populous village.

Rumor had it that it was not only profitable to sell hemp, lard, and leather abroad, but also wheat.

Dobrynin needed a village for export. He wished to expel the peasants to the Kherson Governorate.

1931

A leading figure in the Russian Formalist movement of the 1920s, VIKTOR SHKLOVSKY (1893-1984) had a profound effect on twentieth-century Russian literature. Several of his books have been translated into English, including *Theory of Prose*, *Knight's Move*, and *A Hunt for Optimism*, all available from Dalkey Archive Press.

VALERIYA YERMISHOVA is a freelance translator. She studied French language and literature and economics at State University of New York at Binghamton and picked up translation certificates at NYU and the University of Chicago. She is active in the translation community and served as president-elect and president of the New York Circle of Translators between 2014 and 2016. She currently lives in New York City.

MICHAL AJVAZ, *The Golden Age.*
The Other City.
PIERRE ALBERT-BIROT, *Grabinoulor.*
YUZ ALESHKOVSKY, *Kangaroo.*
FELIPE ALFAU, *Chromos.*
Locos.
JOE AMATO, *Samuel Taylor's Last Night.*
IVAN ÂNGELO, *The Celebration.*
The Tower of Glass.
ANTÓNIO LOBO ANTUNES, *Knowledge of Hell.*
The Splendor of Portugal.
ALAIN ARIAS-MISSON, *Theatre of Incest.*
JOHN ASHBERY & JAMES SCHUYLER, *A Nest of Ninnies.*
ROBERT ASHLEY, *Perfect Lives.*
GABRIELA AVIGUR-ROTEM, *Heatwave and Crazy Birds.*
DJUNA BARNES, *Ladies Almanack.*
Ryder.
JOHN BARTH, *Letters.*
Sabbatical.
DONALD BARTHELME, *The King.*
Paradise.
SVETISLAV BASARA, *Chinese Letter.*
MIQUEL BAUÇÀ, *The Siege in the Room.*
RENÉ BELLETTO, *Dying.*
MAREK BIENCZYK, *Transparency.*
ANDREI BITOV, *Pushkin House.*
ANDREJ BLATNIK, *You Do Understand.*
Law of Desire.
LOUIS PAUL BOON, *Chapel Road.*
My Little War.
Summer in Termuren.
ROGER BOYLAN, *Killoyle.*
IGNÁCIO DE LOYOLA BRANDÃO, *Anonymous Celebrity.*
Zero.
BONNIE BREMSER, *Troia: Mexican Memoirs.*
CHRISTINE BROOKE-ROSE, *Amalgamemnon.*
BRIGID BROPHY, *In Transit.*
The Prancing Novelist.

GERALD L. BRUNS, *Modern Poetry and the Idea of Language.*
GABRIELLE BURTON, *Heartbreak Hotel.*
MICHEL BUTOR, *Degrees.*
Mobile.
G. CABRERA INFANTE, *Infante's Inferno.*
Three Trapped Tigers.
JULIETA CAMPOS, *The Fear of Losing Eurydice.*
ANNE CARSON, *Eros the Bittersweet.*
ORLY CASTEL-BLOOM, *Dolly City.*
LOUIS-FERDINAND CÉLINE, *North.*
Conversations with Professor Y.
London Bridge.
MARIE CHAIX, *The Laurels of Lake Constance.*
HUGO CHARTERIS, *The Tide Is Right.*
ERIC CHEVILLARD, *Demolishing Nisard.*
The Author and Me.
MARC CHOLODENKO, *Mordechai Schamz.*
JOSHUA COHEN, *Witz.*
EMILY HOLMES COLEMAN, *The Shutter of Snow.*
ERIC CHEVILLARD, *The Author and Me.*
ROBERT COOVER, *A Night at the Movies.*
STANLEY CRAWFORD, *Log of the S.S. The Mrs Unguentine.*
Some Instructions to My Wife.
RENÉ CREVEL, *Putting My Foot in It.*
RALPH CUSACK, *Cadenza.*
NICHOLAS DELBANCO, *Sherbrookes.*
The Count of Concord.
NIGEL DENNIS, *Cards of Identity.*
PETER DIMOCK, *A Short Rhetoric for Leaving the Family.*
ARIEL DORFMAN, *Konfidenz.*
COLEMAN DOWELL, *Island People.*
Too Much Flesh and Jabez.
ARKADII DRAGOMOSHCHENKO, *Dust.*
RIKKI DUCORNET, *Phosphor in Dreamland.*
The Complete Butcher's Tales.

RIKKI DUCORNET (cont.), *The Jade Cabinet*.
The Fountains of Neptune.

WILLIAM EASTLAKE, *The Bamboo Bed*.
Castle Keep.
Lyric of the Circle Heart.

JEAN ECHENOZ, *Chopin's Move*.

STANLEY ELKIN, *A Bad Man*.
Criers and Kibitzers, Kibitzers and Criers.
The Dick Gibson Show.
The Franchiser.
The Living End.
Mrs. Ted Bliss.

FRANÇOIS EMMANUEL, *Invitation to a Voyage*.

PAUL EMOND, *The Dance of a Sham*.

SALVADOR ESPRIU, *Ariadne in the Grotesque Labyrinth*.

LESLIE A. FIEDLER, *Love and Death in the American Novel*.

JUAN FILLOY, *Op Oloop*.

ANDY FITCH, *Pop Poetics*.

GUSTAVE FLAUBERT, *Bouvard and Pécuchet*.

KASS FLEISHER, *Talking out of School*.

JON FOSSE, *Aliss at the Fire*.
Melancholy.

FORD MADOX FORD, *The March of Literature*.

MAX FRISCH, *I'm Not Stiller*.
Man in the Holocene.

CARLOS FUENTES, *Christopher Unborn*.
Distant Relations.
Terra Nostra.
Where the Air Is Clear.

TAKEHIKO FUKUNAGA, *Flowers of Grass*.

WILLIAM GADDIS, JR., *The Recognitions*.

JANICE GALLOWAY, *Foreign Parts*.
The Trick Is to Keep Breathing.

WILLIAM H. GASS, *Life Sentences*.
The Tunnel.
The World Within the Word.
Willie Masters' Lonesome Wife.

GÉRARD GAVARRY, *Hoppla! 1 2 3*.

ETIENNE GILSON, *The Arts of the Beautiful*.
Forms and Substances in the Arts.

C. S. GISCOMBE, *Giscome Road*.
Here.

DOUGLAS GLOVER, *Bad News of the Heart*.

WITOLD GOMBROWICZ, *A Kind of Testament*.

PAULO EMÍLIO SALES GOMES, *P's Three Women*.

GEORGI GOSPODINOV, *Natural Novel*.

JUAN GOYTISOLO, *Count Julian*.
Juan the Landless.
Makbara.
Marks of Identity.

HENRY GREEN, *Blindness*.
Concluding.
Doting.
Nothing.

JACK GREEN, *Fire the Bastards!*

JIŘÍ GRUŠA, *The Questionnaire*.

MELA HARTWIG, *Am I a Redundant Human Being?*

JOHN HAWKES, *The Passion Artist*.
Whistlejacket.

ELIZABETH HEIGHWAY, ED., *Contemporary Georgian Fiction*.

AIDAN HIGGINS, *Balcony of Europe*.
Blind Man's Bluff.
Bornholm Night-Ferry.
Langrishe, Go Down.
Scenes from a Receding Past.

KEIZO HINO, *Isle of Dreams*.

KAZUSHI HOSAKA, *Plainsong*.

ALDOUS HUXLEY, *Antic Hay*.
Point Counter Point.
Those Barren Leaves.
Time Must Have a Stop.

NAOYUKI II, *The Shadow of a Blue Cat*.

DRAGO JANČAR, *The Tree with No Name*.

MIKHEIL JAVAKHISHVILI, *Kvachi*.

GERT JONKE, *The Distant Sound*.
Homage to Czerny.
The System of Vienna.

JACQUES JOUET, *Mountain R.*
Savage.
Upstaged.
MIEKO KANAI, *The Word Book.*
YORAM KANIUK, *Life on Sandpaper.*
ZURAB KARUMIDZE, *Dagny.*
JOHN KELLY, *From Out of the City.*
HUGH KENNER, *Flaubert, Joyce and Beckett: The Stoic Comedians.*
Joyce's Voices.
DANILO KIŠ, *The Attic.*
The Lute and the Scars.
Psalm 44.
A Tomb for Boris Davidovich.
ANITA KONKKA, *A Fool's Paradise.*
GEORGE KONRÁD, *The City Builder.*
TADEUSZ KONWICKI, *A Minor Apocalypse.*
The Polish Complex.
ANNA KORDZAIA-SAMADASHVILI, *Me, Margarita.*
MENIS KOUMANDAREAS, *Koula.*
ELAINE KRAF, *The Princess of 72nd Street.*
JIM KRUSOE, *Iceland.*
AYSE KULIN, *Farewell: A Mansion in Occupied Istanbul.*
EMILIO LASCANO TEGUI, *On Elegance While Sleeping.*
ERIC LAURRENT, *Do Not Touch.*
VIOLETTE LEDUC, *La Bâtarde.*
EDOUARD LEVÉ, *Autoportrait.*
Newspaper.
Suicide.
Works.
MARIO LEVI, *Istanbul Was a Fairy Tale.*
DEBORAH LEVY, *Billy and Girl.*
JOSÉ LEZAMA LIMA, *Paradiso.*
ROSA LIKSOM, *Dark Paradise.*
OSMAN LINS, *Avalovara.*
The Queen of the Prisons of Greece.
FLORIAN LIPUŠ, *The Errors of Young Tjaž.*
GORDON LISH, *Peru.*
ALF MACLOCHLAINN, *Out of Focus.*
Past Habitual.

The Corpus in the Library.
RON LOEWINSOHN, *Magnetic Field(s).*
YURI LOTMAN, *Non-Memoirs.*
D. KEITH MANO, *Take Five.*
MINA LOY, *Stories and Essays of Mina Loy.*
MICHELINE AHARONIAN MARCOM, *A Brief History of Yes.*
The Mirror in the Well.
BEN MARCUS, *The Age of Wire and String.*
WALLACE MARKFIELD, *Teitlebaum's Window.*
DAVID MARKSON, *Reader's Block.*
Wittgenstein's Mistress.
CAROLE MASO, *AVA.*
HISAKI MATSUURA, *Triangle.*
LADISLAV MATEJKA & KRYSTYNA POMORSKA, EDS., *Readings in Russian Poetics: Formalist & Structuralist Views.*
HARRY MATHEWS, *Cigarettes.*
The Conversions.
The Human Country.
The Journalist.
My Life in CIA.
Singular Pleasures.
The Sinking of the Odradek.
Stadium.
Tlooth.
HISAKI MATSUURA, *Triangle.*
DONAL MCLAUGHLIN, *beheading the virgin mary, and other stories.*
JOSEPH MCELROY, *Night Soul and Other Stories.*
ABDELWAHAB MEDDEB, *Talismano.*
GERHARD MEIER, *Isle of the Dead.*
HERMAN MELVILLE, *The Confidence-Man.*
AMANDA MICHALOPOULOU, *I'd Like.*
STEVEN MILLHAUSER, *The Barnum Museum.*
In the Penny Arcade.
RALPH J. MILLS, JR., *Essays on Poetry.*
MOMUS, *The Book of Jokes.*
CHRISTINE MONTALBETTI, *The Origin of Man.*
Western.

NICHOLAS MOSLEY, *Accident.*
Assassins.
Catastrophe Practice.
A Garden of Trees.
Hopeful Monsters.
Imago Bird.
Inventing God.
Look at the Dark.
Metamorphosis.
Natalie Natalia.
Serpent.

WARREN MOTTE, *Fables of the Novel:*
French Fiction since 1990.
Fiction Now: The French Novel in the
21st Century.
Mirror Gazing.
Oulipo: A Primer of Potential Literature.

GERALD MURNANE, *Barley Patch.*
Inland.

YVES NAVARRE, *Our Share of Time.*
Sweet Tooth.

DOROTHY NELSON, *In Night's City.*
Tar and Feathers.

ESHKOL NEVO, *Homesick.*

WILFRIDO D. NOLLEDO, *But for*
the Lovers.

BORIS A. NOVAK, *The Master of*
Insomnia.

FLANN O'BRIEN, *At Swim-Two-Birds.*
The Best of Myles.
The Dalkey Archive.
The Hard Life.
The Poor Mouth.
The Third Policeman.

CLAUDE OLLIER, *The Mise-en-Scène.*
Wert and the Life Without End.

PATRIK OUŘEDNÍK, *Europeana.*
The Opportune Moment, 1855.

BORIS PAHOR, *Necropolis.*

FERNANDO DEL PASO, *News from*
the Empire.
Palinuro of Mexico.

ROBERT PINGET, *The Inquisitory.*
Mahu or The Material.
Trio.

MANUEL PUIG, *Betrayed by Rita*
Hayworth.

The Buenos Aires Affair.
Heartbreak Tango.

RAYMOND QUENEAU, *The Last Days.*
Odile.
Pierrot Mon Ami.
Saint Glinglin.

ANN QUIN, *Berg.*
Passages.
Three.
Tripticks.

ISHMAEL REED, *The Free-Lance*
Pallbearers.
The Last Days of Louisiana Red.
Ishmael Reed: The Plays.
Juice!
The Terrible Threes.
The Terrible Twos.
Yellow Back Radio Broke-Down.

JASIA REICHARDT, *15 Journeys Warsaw*
to London.

JOÃO UBALDO RIBEIRO, *House of the*
Fortunate Buddhas.

JEAN RICARDOU, *Place Names.*

RAINER MARIA RILKE,
The Notebooks of Malte Laurids Brigge.

JULIÁN RÍOS, *The House of Ulysses.*
Larva: A Midsummer Night's Babel.
Poundemonium.

ALAIN ROBBE-GRILLET, *Project for a*
Revolution in New York.
A Sentimental Novel.

AUGUSTO ROA BASTOS, *I the Supreme.*

DANIËL ROBBERECHTS, *Arriving in*
Avignon.

JEAN ROLIN, *The Explosion of the*
Radiator Hose.

OLIVIER ROLIN, *Hotel Crystal.*

ALIX CLEO ROUBAUD, *Alix's Journal.*

JACQUES ROUBAUD, *The Form of*
a City Changes Faster, Alas, Than the
Human Heart.
The Great Fire of London.
Hortense in Exile.
Hortense Is Abducted.
Mathematics: The Plurality of Worlds of
Lewis.
Some Thing Black.

RAYMOND ROUSSEL, *Impressions of Africa*.

VEDRANA RUDAN, *Night*.

PABLO M. RUIZ, *Four Cold Chapters on the Possibility of Literature*.

GERMAN SADULAEV, *The Maya Pill*.

TOMAŽ ŠALAMUN, *Soy Realidad*.

LYDIE SALVAYRE, *The Company of Ghosts*.
The Lecture.
The Power of Flies.

LUIS RAFAEL SÁNCHEZ, *Macho Camacho's Beat*.

SEVERO SARDUY, *Cobra & Maitreya*.

NATHALIE SARRAUTE, *Do You Hear Them?*
Martereau.
The Planetarium.

STIG SÆTERBAKKEN, *Siamese*.
Self-Control.
Through the Night.

ARNO SCHMIDT, *Collected Novellas*.
Collected Stories.
Nobodaddy's Children.
Two Novels.

ASAF SCHURR, *Motti*.

GAIL SCOTT, *My Paris*.

DAMION SEARLS, *What We Were Doing and Where We Were Going*.

JUNE AKERS SEESE,
Is This What Other Women Feel Too?

BERNARD SHARE, *Inish*.
Transit.

VIKTOR SHKLOVSKY, *Bowstring*.
Literature and Cinematography.
Theory of Prose.
Third Factory.
Zoo, or Letters Not about Love.

PIERRE SINIAC, *The Collaborators*.

KJERSTI A. SKOMSVOLD,
The Faster I Walk, the Smaller I Am.

JOSEF ŠKVORECKÝ, *The Engineer of Human Souls*.

GILBERT SORRENTINO, *Aberration of Starlight*.
Blue Pastoral.
Crystal Vision.

Imaginative Qualities of Actual Things.
Mulligan Stew. *Red the Fiend*.
Steelwork.
Under the Shadow.

MARKO SOSIČ, *Ballerina, Ballerina*.

ANDRZEJ STASIUK, *Dukla*.
Fado.

GERTRUDE STEIN, *The Making of Americans*.
A Novel of Thank You.

LARS SVENDSEN, *A Philosophy of Evil*.

PIOTR SZEWC, *Annihilation*.

GONÇALO M. TAVARES, *A Man: Klaus Klump*.
Jerusalem.
Learning to Pray in the Age of Technique.

LUCIAN DAN TEODOROVICI,
Our Circus Presents...

NIKANOR TERATOLOGEN, *Assisted Living*.

STEFAN THEMERSON, *Hobson's Island*.
The Mystery of the Sardine.
Tom Harris.

TAEKO TOMIOKA, *Building Waves*.

JOHN TOOMEY, *Sleepwalker*.

DUMITRU TSEPENEAG, *Hotel Europa*.
The Necessary Marriage.
Pigeon Post.
Vain Art of the Fugue.

ESTHER TUSQUETS, *Stranded*.

DUBRAVKA UGRESIC, *Lend Me Your Character*.
Thank You for Not Reading.

TOR ULVEN, *Replacement*.

MATI UNT, *Brecht at Night*.
Diary of a Blood Donor.
Things in the Night.

ÁLVARO URIBE & OLIVIA SEARS, EDS.,
Best of Contemporary Mexican Fiction.

ELOY URROZ, *Friction*.
The Obstacles.

LUISA VALENZUELA, *Dark Desires and the Others*.
He Who Searches.

PAUL VERHAEGHEN, *Omega Minor*.

BORIS VIAN, *Heartsnatcher*.

LLORENÇ VILLALONGA, *The Dolls' Room.*

TOOMAS VINT, *An Unending Landscape.*

ORNELA VORPSI, *The Country Where No One Ever Dies.*

AUSTRYN WAINHOUSE, *Hedyphagetica.*

CURTIS WHITE, *America's Magic Mountain.*
The Idea of Home.
Memories of My Father Watching TV.
Requiem.

DIANE WILLIAMS,
Excitability: Selected Stories.
Romancer Erector.

DOUGLAS WOOLF, *Wall to Wall.*
Ya! & John-Juan.

JAY WRIGHT, *Polynomials and Pollen.*
The Presentable Art of Reading Absence.

PHILIP WYLIE, *Generation of Vipers.*

MARGUERITE YOUNG, *Angel in the Forest.*
Miss MacIntosh, My Darling.

REYOUNG, *Unbabbling.*

VLADO ŽABOT, *The Succubus.*

ZORAN ŽIVKOVIĆ , *Hidden Camera.*

LOUIS ZUKOFSKY, *Collected Fiction.*

VITOMIL ZUPAN, *Minuet for Guitar.*

SCOTT ZWIREN, *God Head.*

AND MORE . . .